Warren S. Belding

Biography of Dr. W. A. Belding

Including sixty years of ministerial pioneer work

Warren S. Belding

Biography of Dr. W. A. Belding
Including sixty years of ministerial pioneer work

ISBN/EAN: 9783337015916

Printed in Europe, USA, Canada, Australia, Japan

Cover: Foto ©Raphael Reischuk / pixelio.de

More available books at **www.hansebooks.com**

BIOGRAPHY

.....OF....

DR. W. A. BELDING,

INCLUDING SIXTY YEARS OF MINISTERIAL
PIONEER WORK.

✢✢✢✢

WRITTEN BY

HIS GRANDSON, W.´S. BELDING.

✢✢✢✢

CINCINNATI, O.:
JOHN F. ROWE, Publisher.
1897.

BIOGRAPHY OF DR. WARREN ASA BELDING.

*Written by His Grandson and Namesake, War-
ren S. Belding, October, 1896.*

This little work is written in response to the
request of numerous friends of my grandfather's.
They have said that there are many persons who,
charmed with what they have seen of the simple
purity and unselfishness of his life, would fain
know more of its details and incidents. No
startling or thrilling adventures have occurred
therein, but the story is of a man of remarkable
abilities in financiering for philanthropic and
Christian work—remarkable also for his success
in evangelizing.

During the sixty-odd years devoted to ministerial work, he has immersed, with his own hands,
between eleven and twelve thousand persons.
Besides this, the raising of funds for colleges and
schools, and the erection of and paying for numerous churches scattered all over this land, has
engaged his time. From Maine to California,
and southward to Florida and Mississippi, there
is hardly a State that has not been the scene of
his labors at some time during his busy life. It
is asserted that no man among the Disciples of
Christ is personally known to as many brethren
as the subject of this sketch.

The record of one year, as shown by its diary,

is remarkable for its results. He was then corre-
sponding secretary of the General Christian Missionary Society, and also its financial agent. That
year he raised twenty thousand dollars in money
and pledges, wrote two thousand letters, received
and read four thousand letters, and traveled about
twenty thousand miles. This is undoubtedly his
greatest year measured by visible results, but
there are several years in which he traveled fully
as much.

If·I succeed in presenting to the reader a true
picture of the character and work of my grandfather, I am satisfied that it will be interesting
reading, especially to those who, by association
with him, have caught a glimpse of the purity,
simplicity and loving kindness which have been
the natural characteristics governing his life.

The writer has had the advantage of access to
his grandfather's diaries, some forty-six in number, covering the entire period from 1850 to the
present year 1896. An idea of the methodical
habits of the doctor may be had when I state that
not a volume is missing. When asked if he could
find his diaries for my use, the response was,
" Yes, sir," and they were immediately produced
in good condition and in consecutive order.

I have also had the good fortune to acquire
some manuscript written by my father, most of
which is from recollections dictated or told by
grandfather in the hours when his mind went
back to his earlier days. Some manuscript from
Bro. Walter S. Hayden is also acknowledged.

He once undertook this work, but gave it up for lack of time.

But last and most helpful of all has been the loving assistance of grandfather himself, without which I doubt not that many mistakes would have been made, as the diaries before spoken of were not designed by their writer to form the basis of a work of this kind; hence many things were omitted which were essential to a full understanding of their contents.

The preparing of this work for publication has been a " labor of love " on my part, and, though hampered by the lack of a literary education, and obliged to write in time taken from my business, still I hope that all may feel repaid for the time spent in its perusal.

WARREN S. BELDING.

INTRODUCTION.

It is well that this book has been written. The life of its central figure spans the entire history of "the current reformation." His ministerial experience dates from an early period in the history of the Disciples of Christ. He was a companion of many of the mighty men who, under God, were agents in the inauguration of a movement for the union of Christians in order to the evangelization of the world by a return, in faith and life, to the religion described on the pages of the New Testament. The incidents in this long and unusually busy life, recorded in this volume, throw not a little light on the early history of the Disciples. To read them will enable one, in imagination, to live in the midst of the stirring scenes of those early years. This will be of practical value. Inspiration to more intelligent and heroic endeavor in behalf of the Christianity of Christ will follow. The time, in our growth, has come for the publication of such records. Too many of our aged men, pioneers in this good work, have passed from earth without telling the story of their trials and triumphs. Our poverty is greater on account of this failure. Such simple narratives will possess, in years to come, great value to the writers of history. Those who are now coming into the work of the ministry, and into the fellowship of the churches of Christ, have, as a rule, an exceedingly imperfect under-

standing of the condition of the body of Christ
in the United States from thirty to sixty or
seventy-five years ago. They are ignorant of
the conditions out of which came the religious
communion known as the Christian Church or
Disciples of Christ. There is therefore a failure
to discern the good hand of. our God, and to realize that this movement is a child of Providence.
The pioneers were mighty men, some of them
mental giants, all of them moral heroes, to whom
was committed, by the Head of the body, Jesus
Christ our Lord, a special message and mission.
No man can fully understand what we call "the
current reformation" who is not acquainted with
the facts connected with its origin. These explain its spirit, purpose, method. The most interesting and effective manner in which these
facts can be exhibited is in the simply written
narratives of personal adventure and experience
by the men who are yet with us, and who were
actors in those "times that tried men's souls."
It is this feature of the following pages that gives
to them their value. It is probable that no man
living among us has delivered so great a number
of sermons, attended a larger number of religious
conventions and conferences, been instrumental
in erecting a larger number of houses of worship,
has a personal acquaintance in more churches,
has solicited money for religious and educational
enterprises to a greater extent, or has baptized
more men and women into Christ, than has the
central figure in this book. His narrative is sim-

ple, clear, veracious. He speaks of matters of
which he was personally cognizant. This volume
ought to be widely circulated and read, especially
by the middle-aged and the young. The elderly
folks will find pleasure in these pages, because
their contents will remind them of a glorious
past—a period of time in the remembrance of
which they find a peculiar joy.

B. B. TYLER.

INTRODUCTORY.

The honest record of the experiences of many years of those who have served God well in any noble ministries in his work among men, especially if these ministries have been full of unbroken active service, is of inestimable value to the Church. There is offered to us in such a record the full harvest of a life of true faith, of exalted motives, of a sincere devotion to the cause of our Master, of unwavering fidelity to the holiest convictions that can inspire human souls. The story of such a life, even if passed in the least ambitious paths, is a picture that can be studied with pleasure and profit Such unostentatious "annals" of a long service in the Church of God are unfolded to us in the pages of this book. Personally familiarly acquainted, I may say, with Dr. Belding's history for about fifty-seven years, I can speak with confidence of what it reports to us. I desire to point out some particular features of this history.

Dr. Belding throughout all his life has been unfalteringly true to his profession as a Christian. The ardent faith of his early years has sustained him, a faith unchanged, unabated to the present hour. There have been no periods of weakening or defection in his life. His clear conceptions of New Testament Christianity also, which he learned directly from the fathers of our reformatory movement, have never, even for a moment, given way before the influence of any of the adverse changes which time inevitably brings with it. Our brother holds fast to-day, close on the borders of four-score years, as he did in his youth, to the faith, the doctrine and the practice of New Testament Christianity. This the pages of this book reveal.

The author of these personal memoirs has always been ardent and zealous in whatever service he undertook. To be constantly in action has been an enduring passion with him. This is high praise, that is not due to all in the ministry, but it is a most noble instinct of the soul.

As this biography relates, Dr. Belding has been in many forms of the Master's service. He has been very active in our national and State missionary and benevolent enterprises, and has always courageously urged upon churches and individuals their full duty to support the cause of Christ, and in a manner that gave him much success, and never caused him to lose the good will of the people. His experience has been large in "setting in order the things that were wanting" in churches, and in quieting disturbances and restoring peace among brethren. To him is due this great praise: *he never made trouble any-where.* The reason of this is, that he has been a man of kindly disposition and of wisdom. Dr. Belding has not been a blunderer.

But I have said enough. My object in these introductory words is to tell the reader what kind of a man he is who here tells the story of his life, and consequently what is the value of the book he has written.

CHARLES LOUIS LOOS.

LEXINGTON, Ky.

TABLE OF CONTENTS.

(XIII)

BIOGRAPHY OF DR. W. A. BELDING.

CHAPTER I.

HENRY WARD BEECHER, being once asked what things were necessary to a noble and successful life, replied: "First let a man choose a good father and mother." The influence of ancestral habits and training can be traced in the life of every man, and it is certainly a point in a man's favor that we can trace his ancestry back to the old States of Massachusetts and Connecticut. If it was "the land of witches," it was also "the land of steady habits." If the unbending rigor of conscience led the Puritan Fathers to a too literal interpretation of the command, "Suffer not a witch to live," they were certainly no more given to superstition than the rest of the world at that time; while for unyielding loyalty to conviction and devotion to truth, as they understood it, they have probably never been surpassed.

The genealogy of the Belding family has been traced by the writer back eight generations, to a Richard Bayldon, of Wethersfield, Conn., living in 1640. Further back than this it is difficult to go, but the name is undoubtedly English. Some branches of the family have changed the spelling to *Beldin*, *Belden*, or *Beldon;* but it is certain that the original spelling was *Bayldon*, and the first change, to *Belding*.

Dr. Rufus Belding, the father of W. A. Beld-

ing, was born in Northampton, Mass., in 1777.
The year 1800 found him and his wife—Charlotte
Sabin, daughter of Jeremiah Sabin, of Northampton—in company with a large number of
others, who emigrated about that time from Massachusetts and Connecticut to various portions of
what was then called the Connecticut Western
Reserve, but which soon after became a portion
of the State of Ohio.

The party with which the family traveled went
first to Cleveland, O., then but a village of seven
log cabins. It is difficult for us to realize how
new and undeveloped that region then was. Only
four years previous (July 4, 1796), the first sur-
veying party of the Western Reserve had landed
at the mouth of Conneaut Creek, and on July
22, of the same year, the city of Cleveland was
founded. Every part of the ground upon which
that city is now built could have been purchased
for one dollar and a quarter per acre at the time
the doctor and his family arrived.

The subject of this sketch says his father had
some intention of settling there and beginning
the practice of medicine, for which he had prepared ; but, after looking the ground over, he
decided that it was too unhealthy even for a physician. Accordingly he wended his way to what
is now Randolph, Portage Co., O. Accompany-
ing him were two other families, named Baker
and Blackman ; the Bakers settled in Shalersville
and the Blackmans in Aurora. It was difficult to
travel through the almost unbroken wilderness, as

for miles it was necessary to cut their way through the dense forests.

Upon his arrival, he set about making a home. Here he afterwards lived fifty-seven years, in that time witnessing the vast changes produced in the wilderness around him by the settling of thousands of immigrants from the Eastern States.

He continued the practice of medicine until ill health compelled him to abandon it, leaving a record of which few physicians can boast — that he never was accused of being exorbitant in his charges. When asked why he did so much work for so little pay, he often replied: "It is hard enough to be sick without having to pay out all one has for the privilege." Devoting himself to others, with little thought of compensation, it follows naturally that he left only a small property to his numerous family at his death, which occurred in 1854.

The wife, who bravely shared with him the dangers and privations of this pioneer life, was born in Herkimer County, N. Y. Her maiden name was Charlotte Sabin. She died before Warren was two years old, leaving eight children —six older and one younger than he. The boys were Justin, Sabin, Anson and Alvin; the sisters, Louisa, Ruth and Charlotte.

CHAPTER II.

WARREN ASA BELDING was born at Randolph, September 5, 1816, about sixteen years after his parents settled in that place. There must have been much of the pioneer vigor in the constitution of the lad, for that life in a new country was trying enough at best; but, for one deprived of a mother's love and care before his second birthday anniversary, it must have been doubly hard.

One little occurrence of this early time in his life's history remains engraven on his memory and suggests the difficulties under which the father labored in endeavoring to care for the motherless children. This incident is rather amusing in the light of his religious experiences of after years.

Shortly after his mother's death, his father took him on horseback to the house of a good old Presbyterian deacon, who had kindly offered to take care of the lad for a time. As they drew up at the door of the good man's cabin, he made his appearance, wearing a countenance which the doctor declares was as "[long as the moral law," and which made such an impression on his mind that for years he associated solemn countenances with Presbyterianism.

In the family of this man Warren remained for some time, and, as he grew up, he visited them often. The deacon had a very kind heart, but was of a strong-willed, unbending nature, and was a firm Calvinist of the old school. It was from this family that Warren first learned of the conflict between Calvinism and Arminianism. Indeed, it furnished in itself a living example of that conflict !

For many years Presbyterianism had held un-disputed sway in that section, but, not long before the events just spoken of, the Methodists (who were at that time looked upon much as the Salva-tion Army is to-day) had established a class in the northern part of the town. On a "Sabbath" morning the devoted deacon would saddle his best horse and start for the south, where stood his church ; while his equally devoted and conscien-tious wife would mount the horse saddled for her use, and, giving it free rein and choice, would find the "Spirit" guiding her toward the north, to the Methodist meeting at the schoolhouse. So matters continued for thirty years, both going their separate ways on Sunday, and living the balance of the week in perfect harmony.

"What," says Warren, "I could not under-stand at the time, and have never been quite able to figure out, was why the self-same Spirit who foreordained that the deacon should go south to worship with the Calvinists, should have unerr-ingly led his wife to the north, to worship among the Methodists. I am unable to reconcile it with Christ's prayer, 'That they all may be one ; as thou, Father, art in me, and I in thee ; that they also may be one in us : that the world may know that thou hast sent me.'"

It had been necessary to find homes for Warren's brothers and sisters in different families, and, in consequence, they became almost strangers to one another for a time. But the family was partially reunited by the second marriage of the father, who found a helpmeet in the person of Mrs. Hannah Spellman. By this marriage a daughter, Martha, was born. The second wife lived but a few years, and, after a suitable period of mourning, the father again married. This bride was also a widow, Mrs. Sarah Humphrey. From this marriage but one child was born, Edwin Clinton.

Warren has often declared that it was given to this family to disprove two adages: First, that "there is no such person as a *good stepmother*"; second, that "no house is large enough for two families."

The Widow Spellman had seven children, and the Widow Humphrey two, by their former husbands. There were in this family, as it was finally constituted, five sets of children—nineteen in all—and it is the assertion of the subject of this sketch that few families, if any, ever lived more happily together.

The last wife survived her husband many years, dying at last at the age of eighty-four, at the home of her son, Edwin C. Belding, of Ravenna, O.

CHAPTER III.

Of Warren's own brothers and sisters, all but one (Sabin) attained to maturity. Justin, the oldest, was for nearly forty years engaged in a mercantile business in Randolph, where his life was ended. Anson studied medicine and had just begun to practice in Newburg, O. (now a part of the city of Cleveland), when he] was suddenly stricken by death.

Alvin, the fourth son, and next older than Warren, devoted his life to the medical profession. His last thirty-nine years were spent in Ravenna, O., where he gained a widespread reputation as a skillful physician. He was attacked by typhoid pneumonia ; and, when it was decided that the issue would be fatal, he requested that his brother Warren should be sent for. A telegram was immediately dispatched, but before Warren arrived death had claimed its victim. Alvin, knowing the hours of arrival of the different trains, would often inquire whether the time was not near at hand. At length he said, " I can not wait longer ; bid him good-by for me," and he fell asleep.

In early life Alvin had been skeptical. When (in 1854) he was standing with his brother Warren at the grave of their father, as the remains were being lowered, Alvin said : " I would give the world, if I possessed it, for the hope that you have, and that I have no doubt you enjoy ; but the future looks dark to me." As the years

(7)

passed, his skepticism gradually gave way, until, later, when visited by Warren, he would often invite him to return thanks at the table, and sometimes to read the Scriptures and offer prayer before retiring for the night.

In the autumn preceding his death, while the two were conversing upon religious matters, he said: "You think I will never unite with the church, but I think I shall. If you could know how hard it is for a man of my age to break away from his lifelong associations, you could not be too thankful that you became a Christian in early life. Would that I had done the same!"

Of the sisters, Louisa became the wife of D. K. Wheeler, while Ruth became Mrs. Calvin Rawson. The third, Charlotte, married Joseph H. Ward.

The three sisters lived and died in their native county. Of the original family, none survive except Warren.

At an early age there appeared some of the traits that have since become marked characteristics. Among these were a love of a trade, and a general capacity for business. He relates a number of transactions, which, perhaps, do not differ greatly from the average country boy's experience. But one was of so unique a character that it certainly deserves to be recorded.

A very dear friend of nearly the same age had a name that Warren admired more than any other proper name. He says he tried to purchase it, and to exchange for it, but without success

Finally his business tact suggested that each should take the first name of the other and use it for a second name.   As this met with Asa's favor, they were known thereafter as Asa Warren Rawson and Warren Asa Belding.

Another prominent trait which appeared early in life and which, though subdued by age, has never been lost, is his love for a joke.

One day, while riding—according to custom, upon horseback behind his father—he suddenly called out: "Father, who is that coming behind us on a white horse?"

The father turned himself on his horse, and, looking back, replied: "I see no one."

"Turn your horse around."

This was soon done.   Still the father saw no one.   At this the boy said: "It's just an April fool, father."

This was too much for the serious-minded parent, and the rebuke he administered was so severe that a like experiment was never again attempted at his father's expense.

CHAPTER IV.

At the age of fourteen, Warren was placed in what was called the High School of Randolph. Here he distinguished himself for a time by his high spirits and intense love of fun. He himself says of this period: "I was not as well qualified to enter this school as I might have been had I been as faithful to my studies as I was diligent at play. I do not think I was vindictive, sullen or stubborn, but I *would have* fun."

The boundless energy displayed in after years in the service of Christ found its outlet while he was a boy in the hundreds of mischievous pranks that he played.

Schoolmasters in those days were literally "knights of the birch," and, as it was the standing rule with his father to duplicate any whipping he received at school, Warren considered it a fortunate day when he came off with no more than two punishments. On one occasion, the teacher having remarked many times that he had eyes in the back of his head, it occurred to Warren to test the truth of the remark by removing his chair as he started to sit down. Watching his opportunity, he did so, and, as the result, the teacher measured his length upon the floor. The result may be left to the reader's imagination; but the next day found him as deeply in mischief as ever.

The teacher one day fell asleep in his chair. Warren coolly split a goose-quill, crept softly up, and placed it firmly on the end of his nose. This was too much for the school; the shouts of laughter aroused the slumberer and his ungovernable temper. His first inquiry was: " Who did it?" The scholars were disposed to shield the perpetrator of the daring joke; but the teacher's anger was excited to its fighting-point, and he declared that he would flog every scholar in the school unless the culprit was revealed to him. By some means he gained the desired information, and the truthfulness of the saying that "a scolding does not hurt and a whipping doesn't last long" proved less true in practice than in theory.

Another characteristic, which manifested itself in boyhood, and which has always been prominent in the man, is an ambition not to be outdone. This is not associated with a selfish spirit, nor is it the result of pride, but, rather, the outworking of a restless energy. This quality sometimes led the lad into difficulties. In those days every one drank liquor. Farmers furnished strong drink in the field and at all house and barn raisings. Church-members distilled and sold it without any qualms of conscience and without losing the respect of their neighbors; even ministers of the gospel made liberal use of it. It need not be thought strange that Dr. Rufus Belding had combined hotel-keeping with his farming and practice of medicine. In his hotel, as a matter of course, he kept a bar. Nor was it deemed incongruous that Captain Hubbard, who was one of the leading men of the place, and a deacon in the church, should own and operate a distillery.

As Warren advanced in years he felt an increasing desire to be a man and to do the things that all men seemed to do. Inasmuch as all his male acquaintances drank liquor, he felt that a long stride toward manhood would be taken when he learned to drink. He told his stepmother one day that he wished she would not stint him, but for once give him all the whisky he could take. She immediately granted his request, placing before him a large glass of liquor, well sweetened. Telling him to help himself, she left him. This he proceeded to do, taking spoonful doses and after each one trying to walk a crack in the floor. This was continued until, unable to stand, he fell violently, striking his head and causing his nose to bleed copiously.

A short time after this, he was invited by Captain Hubbard's sons to visit their father's distillery. Obtaining permission from his father, he did so, and was much interested in the various processes of the still. At length one of the boys proposed a test which he said was put to all visitors to the establishment. It was to see who could drink the most of the raw spirits without staggering under the load. The noble sons of the captain set the example of draining the proof-glass filled from the barrel, and Warren, of course, followed suit, emptying several glasses in his anxiety to show his manhood. The consequence was that he became drunk, and had to be carried home in a carriage by his comrades and put to bed to sleep off the effects of the liquor.

·Warren declares from that event he first learned the close relationship existing between falsehood, deceit and the liquor business; for he afterwards learned that the boys who had led in this exploit did not drink a drop, but merely feigned to do so. From that day to this he has declared his undying enmity to the making and sale of intoxicants. He has never swerved from the resolution then formed. The cause of temperance has always found in him a zealous advocate, while the' ranks of total abstainers received a lifelong recruit.

His first literary production, which was read before the school not long afterward, was an essay, in which he took the position that the manufacturers and venders of liquor were more guilty than the consumers; inasmuch as the former acted for the sake of paltry gain, while the drinker oftentimes was the victim of an uncontrollable appetite.

This was a very advanced position for those days, and was vigorously resented by many in the community. One good man, a liquor-dealer and a deacon in the church, forbade his daughter's walking to and from school with a boy of so radical sentiments.

Warren also tried tobacco once—and once only. He has often been heard to say that he does not understand how Christian men can indulge in so filthy and injurious a habit, directly contrary to Second Corinthians vii. 1.

CHAPTER V.

ABOUT this time the doctrine called "Campbellism" was introduced into Randolph. This greatly disturbed the orthodox citizens of the town, so that even the Methodists, who so lately had met with the same disfavor on making their *debut*, took fright, and, joining forces with the Presbyterians, thought to stay the ravages of a delusion which threatened the ruin of many of their best citizens.

The adjoining town of Deerfield had taken hold of the pernicious and unheard-of doctrine, that *God had so plainly and simply revealed his will in the Bible that men of common understanding could read it, gather its meaning, and even tell to others the plan of salvation.* This was astonishing, and led to more Bible reading in a few months than had been done before in many years. Men were sent over from Deerfield, one after another, or in couples, until the wonder was whether all its men were not preachers. These men were Jonas Hartzell, Peter Hartzell, John McGowen, Peter McGowen, Amos Allerton and Z. Finch, with others whose names are not recalled. Most of them found a temporary home at Dr. Belding's, where they were always welcome. One of them, being asked by the doctor how many preachers there were in Deerfield, replied: "About sixty." "How many members in the church?" "About sixty male members."

This was in harmony with Scripture teaching,

(14)

as found in Paul's second letter to Timothy : "The
things thou hast heard . . . commit thou to faithful men, who shall be able to teach others also."

On August 27, 1832, Warren resolved to carry
into execution a desire long cherished, although
expressed to very few ; that desire was to become
a Christian.   His most intimate friend, Stephen R.
Hubbard, had asked him several times to obey the
gospel with him, but Warren was not then ready.
Now that he had made up his mind, he would like
the company of his friend ; however, Stephen's
time and opportunity were past, his desires having
taken another direction.   So Warren alone, true to
his convictions of duty, was immersed, upon a profession of his faith in Christ as the Son of the
living God, by the hands of Elder Marcus Bos-
worth.

The day he was baptized was a memorable one
to the Disciples of Christ in Ohio, as well as to
himself—memorable to the Church as the date of
the first annual meeting of the State.   The pres-
ence of *every leader* and nearly every member of
the denomination living in Ohio made the occasion important to all.

Among those best known who were assembled
on that day were Alexander Campbell ; Tolbert
Fanning, of Tennessee ; A. S. Hayden, William
Hayden, J. J. Moss, and Marcus and Cyrus Bos-
worth.

He cast in his lot with the little company of
Disciples, then nicknamed " Campbellites," although they acknowledged no names except those

sanctioned by the primitive church—"Disciples of Christ," or "Christians." As a church or body, they desired only the name authorized by the Master, when he said that he would build upon a foundation against which the gates of hell could not prevail ; meaning the Church of Christ.

Very naturally, the reader will want to know what became of Stephen Hubbard. His refusal to go with Warren sealed his fate ; from that time forward he never again felt " almost persuaded." He married a devoted and religious young lady ; children were born to them, and the wife, by her devotion to the cause of Jesus, won other souls to him. But her tears and prayers were unavailing in Stephen's behalf. When on her death-bed, she took from beneath her pillow her long-loved Bible —her mother's gift—and begged him to accept it and to promise that, as it had been her guide through life, so he would make it his. He took the well-worn book, but he withheld the promise. The last word heard from him by his old companion was a letter written with the trembling hand of age and betraying the skepticism still nursed in his almost pulseless breast.

Warren, with fixed purpose, began his religious life in earnest. He made an effort several times to speak in prayer-meeting, but each time failed, owing to his extreme embarrassment.

No doubt one reason for this lay in the fact that his former associates had said sneeringly : " Yes, he got dipped that he might be a preacher." The remark had its influence, and, with all his efforts.

to drive it away or rise above it, he was unable for a long time to accomplish what he otherwise might have done.

An incident of this period will illustrate the degree of his embarrassment; and few have felt it more than he. Calling one day on a very pious member of the church—who, to all appearances, was near the close of life, being so feeble that he was unable to speak above a whisper—he was beckoned to the old man's bedside, and, in scarcely audible voice, was requested to pray; but so embarrassed was the lad that he turned aside, feigning not to hear. The good man died soon afterwards, and for a long time Warren was troubled by night and day. He never found relief until he sought pardon of the Lord, resolving that he would never again be guilty of a like offense.

By repeated efforts to speak, this timidity was gradually overcome. A constant study of the Scriptures gave him courage and increased his knowledge of the truth.

CHAPTER VI.

IN January, 1834, accompanied by Stephen Hubbard—who now took no interest in the subject of religion—he one day left the heated schoolroom, and, rushing, boylike, into the extremely cold outdoor air, ran a mile and a quarter to his home. Having become intensely heated by this violent exercise, and using no precaution, they cooled off too rapidly. Warren, as a result, was attacked with a severe cold, and that night was stricken with pneumonia. This disease held him poised between life and death for seven long weeks. Much of that time he was unconscious of his surroundings; but his mind seemed to rove among the stars, from world to world, even to that home of which we know so little, save what we see by the eye of faith! This was told him by his bedside watchers. When consciousness returned, it was decided that there was no hope of life. There were several consulting physicians, partly because of sympathy for the father, who, you will remember, was a physician. Some of them were very confident in their opinions, and said that he "was no better off than in his grave."

The watchfulness of the loving father and the vigilance of the kind-hearted stepmother can never be forgotten. The brothers and sisters also rendered what assistance they could, and, prompted by grief and sympathy, did all that human hands could do to be helpful in these trying hours. The time came when it was thought

the struggle was over. The father had pronounced him dead, and the family was in tears;
while the son, with mind unclouded, was wonder-
ing all the time why the living should manifest so
much grief at so happy a change. He was be-
holding, as in a panorama, his entire life at a
single glance, and at the same time getting a view
of heaven, with its myriads of inhabitants, when,
to his great disappointment, he heard his father
say: "He is reviving."

No language can express the peculiar emotions
of that hour in being brought back to life. The
entire past and the heavenly future, both occupy-
ing the mind at the same moment, are indescribable.
If that point of exquisite bliss can ever again be
reached, it will not, it can not, seem hard to die.

This was the crisis, from which hour he became
convalescent. "A walking skeleton" was re-
ported to infest the house. Long and tedious was
the process of recovery; but precious hours for
study and reflection were afforded, and it was at
this time that he resolved to devote the future of
his life to the proclamation of God's own plan for
the salvation of men, through the gospel of his
Son.

A plan was formed and an effort made to carry
the same into execution. He was to enter the
field in company with A. S. Hayden, his senior
by a few years. When the desire was made
known to his father it did not meet his approval,
and for awhile it was abandoned.

His father was not yet identified with the Disci-

ples, but avowed himself a "Campbellite." He
had been associated with the Universalists, in
which faith his first wife, the mother of Warren,
had lived and died. Her funeral services had
been conducted by Ebenezer Williams, who afterwards became a preacher among the Disciples, as
did also his brother Frederick. Both of them
have told the writer that when they first heard the
ordinance of Christian baptism discussed by the
Disciples, to their minds it was clearly taught,
and their love for Christ and reverence for his authority led them at once to say: "Lord, lead and
we will follow." They were both baptized, believing as firmly as ever that God would ultimately
bring the entire race into a state of holiness and
happiness. They soon lost their belief in Universalism, but when or how they never knew.

To return to the avowal of the father that he
was a Campbellite: he wrote and circulated a
subscription to build a house, in which the people
called "Campbellites" or "Disciples" might
worship. On being asked whether he and one of
his neighbors were Disciples, he promptly answered: "No, we are 'Campbellites.'" He defined the word as meaning one who believes the
teaching of Alexander Campbell, but does not
obey it. He said, further, that that teaching of the
Disciples was the only consistent Scriptural doctrine he had ever heard. He circulated the subscription and largely superintended the work of
building the house, until it was ready for use. He

was among the first within its walls to make confession of his faith in a once crucified and buried,
but now risen and exalted, Savior. His course of
life, in some respects, was changed; in many others there was no need of change. As already
stated, two of the deacons of the church were
manufacturers of whisky; of which he himself
was a retailer. Nevertheless, three better men
would have been hard to find.

The son, Warren, dissuaded by his father from
devoting his life to preaching, and especially from
beginning at so early an age, turned his attention
to the study of medicine. His father had a good
medical library for the times, and he inherited a
taste for this kind of study that increased as the
years rolled on. But, in spite of his love for the
study of medicine, he never lost his desire to
preach the gospel. If an opportunity offered to
talk on the subject, he seldom let it pass without
trying to improve it. It was not, however, until
several years later that he attempted to preach a
discourse. Warren began the practice of medicine in 1839, at Aurora, O., with Dr. Fowler, of
that place, but soon after removed to Greentown,
Stark Co., O.

Being in Wayne County, where Dr. George W.
Lucy was holding a meeting of some days' dura-
tion, the doctor insisted that "Bro. Belding
should preach in his stead." Warren naturally
declined, saying that he had never tried to preach;
but the preaching doctor was not to be put off,

and declared that Warren must do it. When he found excuses of no avail, he made up his mind to make the effort, but told Dr. Lucy that the responsibility of failure lay with him. It is related that he spoke earnestly for about thirty minutes, but when he sat down he could not recollect anything he had said.

Not long after this, while living in Stark County, O., Warren heard a Methodist preacher, one Sunday evening, advance some sentiments which he did not think in harmony with Bible teaching He arose, and begged the privilege of asking a question or two.

It was readily granted by the minister, a Mr. Weekly. The first question was: "Suppose a man to be so depraved by nature that he can not think a good thought, speak a good word, or do a good act, without some renewing grace; if he never gets the renewing grace, on whom does the blame rest?"

Before the question was fairly put, an old gentleman, in a very excited and angry manner, jumped up and said: "I think you had better sit down." Bro. Weekly spoke up very pleasantly, and said: "Speak on, doctor." He resumed his talk, when the old man again cried out: "You had better sit down. You have manifested enough of the spirit of antichrist." Bro. Weekly kindly said, "Go on, brother," keeping silence while the doctor finished his speech. It was a dear speech for him from a business standpoint, as he did not receive a call from a single member of that church for the next three or four months. When a physician's services were needed, they sent ten miles for a Methodist doctor. This was no new thing, however, for "*our religion*" was frequently a persecuted religion. But the world moved on, and the cause of the Master gained friends by being persecuted.

CHAPTER VII.

DOCTOR BELDING, as he was thereafter called, grew in spiritual strength, and was embolden to speak publicly and advocate the distinctive features of the plea which is characteristic of the Disciples of Christ. While in Stark County, he was invited to assist in holding a meeting at Indian Run, where the Baptists had a small church. The pastor, Israel Belton, came in and took a friendly part in the services a few times, until his brethren found so much fault with him that he frankly told them that if they did not cease their persecutions he would unite with the Disciples, for he believed they had the truth. This he subsequently did, and, through the united efforts of Bros. Belton and Belding, the two bodies became one, and have continued thus until the present time.

His professional business frequently called him into adjoining towns, where he would make an appointment to preach in the evening, returning to his home after meeting. Thus he would deliver more discourses in the year than many men who gave their entire time to the work of preaching.

He could never understand how some pastors, making it the business of their lives, could expect the Master to say, "Well done, good and faithful servant," for the little labor they had performed.

We will step back to relate a few incidents which occurred before this time. On September 29, 1837, he was married to Miss Myra E. Ward, the eldest daughter of Elisha Ward, of Randolph, O. Their first-born child, a daughter named Sarah Sophia, died at the age of two years and a half, at Hanover, Columbiana Co., O., where they had taken up their residence. While living at Hanover, he preached throughout Columbiana and Carroll Counties.

While attending an annual meeting in what was called the Roudabush settlement, upon his return from meeting one evening, Mother Roudabush, who spoke very broken English, not knowing that Dr. Belding was in the house, asked: "Who vas dot ugly mon vat breached to-day?" Not being able to describe him very accurately, she was delighted when the doctor stepped into the room, and shouted: "Dot is de werry feller."

A discussion was carried on for several days by Bro. J. H. Lamphear and Dr. Belding on one side, and A. C. Hanger and Dr. Hays, of the Christian Connection, on the other. This attracted much attention in the community, and brought together large audiences. The questions discussed were: "Does the guilt of original sin cleave to every child of Adam?" and, if so, "Does God, by some supernatural interposition of his Spirit, convert and save him?" Of these two propositions Mr. Hanger and Dr. Hays affirmed and the others denied. Another subject was: "Do the Scriptures teach that the alien or sinner must be baptized in order to become a citizen of the kingdom of Christ?" Also: "Are all spiritual blessings promised, in the Bible, *in Christ?*"

These latter propositions were affirmed by Lamp-hear and the Doctor, and denied by the others. This was the first public discussion in which Dr. Belding ever engaged. But the triumph of truth was so apparent to the minds of the people, and they were so demonstrative, that it emboldened him to stand for its defense wherever and whenever it seemed to be demanded of him.

Soon after this, in company with Joseph Rhodes, or Father Rhodes, as he was familiarly called in the community, he went into Carroll County to attend a meeting to be conducted by Bro. Jonas Lamb. The preacher failing to appear, the brethren insisted that Dr. Belding should conduct the meeting — a thing he had never before attempted. But, as he had pledged himself never to shrink from what seemed to be his duty, he said: "With your help and the help of the Lord, I will try." At the first meeting, Saturday afternoon, three persons came forward to confess their faith in the Savior, and asked to be baptized.

Now came a greater ordeal than any preceding one. He had never administered the rite of baptism, and there was doubt in his mind whether it was proper for him to do so, never having been ordained to the ministry. But the thought from the "Book of all books," that every Christian is a "king and priest to God," settled the question, and he resolved to do the best that he could.

The hour was set for the baptism, and a large gathering was in waiting at the water when he arrived. It seemed to him that every eye was fixed upon him, and that everybody knew this to be his first experience. Some, indeed, hoped that he might make a failure, for the people of this community had little regard for the institution. After invoking the divine blessing upon the candidates and administrator, they descended with trembling steps into the water. When a sufficient depth was reached, in as solemn and reverential a manner as possible the person was buried in the baptismal grave, raised from it, and led to the shore with a relief of mind which is easy to imagine. The second candidate was led forward and both went down into the water. The first was so easily baptized that, not being on his guard, he failed to entirely submerge the second, who was very tall. He had partly raised him out of the water, when Father Rhodes shouted: "Bro. Belding, bury that man!" On this advice, he was again lowered into the water and buried. This, while it was very embarrassing, taught him a lesson which he never forgot. Thenceforward he never failed to bury the candidate entrusted to his hands as baptist.

Some years after this, a gentleman in Cato, N. Y., who all his life had been troubled with skepticism, was compelled to yield to the claims of the gospel and desired to be baptized. As he was being led down into the stream, he asked the doctor to bury him as deeply as possible and hold him under the water at least thirty seconds. This request was complied with, and the brethren on shore became quite excited, thinking that perhaps the doctor had not strength to raise him.   Bro. Cook, an elder in the congregation, stepped into the water and was coming to his assistance ; but, before he reached the spot, the apparent struggle was over and the anxiety relieved.

The reason afterward given for this singular request was a desire to remain under water long enough to think of the death, burial and resurrection of Christ.

From this time forward, he devoted much more time than before to preaching, and, while he continued the practice of medicine, he did not, and would not, accept compensation for his service as a preacher.   In looking over his old diaries, we find recorded : " For two hundred and sixty-seven days, spent largely in preaching, I received two dollars and thirty-seven cents in cash, a pair of socks and a pair of striped mittens, knit and given me by an old sister."

CHAPTER VIII.

LEAVING Hanover, he moved to Minerva, Stark County, in 1841. Here he entered into partnership with Bro. Geo. W. Lucy, who was also a physician and preacher. Being alike interested both in the practice of medicine and in preaching the gospel, they so managed that one of them was constantly filling a pulpit on Lord's-days, and frequently engaged in protracted meetings during the week.

Bro. J. H. Jones was assisting in a meeting in Minerva, where he and the doctor were preaching alternately. One afternoon, when Bro. Jones was expected to preach, the hour for meeting arrived, but the preacher did not put in an appearance. The brethren, becoming somewhat impatient, requested Dr. Belding to go on with the services. After the opening hymn, the reading of the Scriptures and prayer, and after the doctor had announced the subject of his discourse, Bro. Jones stepped in the door. Dr. Belding sat down, and Bro. Jones, wiping the freely flowing perspiration from his face, walked into the pulpit and said: " Brethren, I have been a-fishing ; and no man can be a good preacher who is not a good fisherman." He then continued : "Jesus once said, ' Follow me, and I will make you fishers of men.' Pray tell me, where did a man ever catch a fish but in the water?''

This was the theme of his discourse, founded upon the language of Christ to Nicodemus, John

iii. 5 : "Except a man be born of water and of
the Spirit, he can not enter into the kingdom of
God." He gave an explanation of the figurative
language of the Savior, as follows : "The man begotten or regenerated by the Spirit, through the instrumentality of the gospel, as Paul declares (1 Cor.
iv. 15) : ' Though ye have ten thousand instructors
in Christ, yet have ye not many fathers : for in Christ
Jesus I have begotten you through the gospel '—
this man, being baptized, or born of water (not of
a *few drops*, a substance less than itself, but a
burial, a *planting*, an *overwhelming*), is born of
the Spirit at the same time, having been begotten
by it. It is one thing to become a citizen of a
kingdom, but quite another to form the character
of a loyal citizen. The King will crown only
those who are loyal."

While speaking of the peculiarities of J. H. Jones
(for there has never been one like him), we will
relate another incident which occurred at Minerva
in the same meeting. While Bro. Jones was
preaching, one of his own little boys, who had
been led into the meeting by his aunt, his mother
being absent that day, partaking of his father's
mischievous disposition, seemed inclined to take
advantage of circumstances. While his father
was preaching, he did not behave himself in a
manner altogether satisfactory. His father spoke
to him reprovingly two or three times without
producing the desired result. Thereupon he
asked the congregation to sing a few verses of a
familiar hymn, and, stepping down from the pul-

pit, he took the offending lad by the hand and started toward the door.   Conviction at once seized the boy, and, if drops of grief are an evidence of repentance, he became a true penitent. Nevertheless, his father chastised him with a hickory switch.   The performance being ended, the lad was brought in and seated, with an emphatic "Sit down and behave yourself."   After this episode, the preacher resumed his place in the pulpit, and succeeded (as few men can do) in drawing the attention of the people from what had occurred, to the subject under discussion.

The following anecdote will illustrate the danger of indiscriminate rebuke from the pulpit: A minister, who was called to preach in a certain place, found before him a young man who not only seemed indifferent to the sermon, but who was talking and apparently trying to attract the attention of those around him.   The speaker rebuked him sharply, but without good result. When the preacher went to his temporary home, the host expressed his regret that he had reproved the young man ; for he belonged to one of the best families in town, but was an *idiot* — not responsible for what he did — and the parents would be much grieved.   The preacher declared that thereafter he never dared to reprove any one in church for fear of rebuking an idiot.

The doctor thought on one occasion that he would try the effect of relating the above incident in church.   It was while holding a meeting at Cascade, Mich.   Two young ladies — one the daughter of a clergyman in the village, the other an intimate associate of hers—had proved very troublesome, not only to the resident pastors, but to all who had filled the pulpits of the place. After inquiring who they were, and being told that it would be useless to reprove them, the doctor one day paused in the midst of his sermon and told the story. It proved effectual as nothing else had been. The girls covered their faces with their veils and pouted until the services were over. They then said they would not hear that man preach again, because he had *called them idiots*. He frankly confessed that it would have been much better to interest them and captivate their affections, if possible, by the gospel of Christ, and lead them to an acknowledgment of the truth. But this appeared to be hopeless.

About the year 1840, the doctor held a series of meetings at Wintersville, O. In the course of the protracted effort a number of persons confessed Christ and desired baptism. The same difficulty was encountered, to a limited extent, which is often urged by pedobaptists as an argument against immersion, viz.: the scarcity of water. There was no convenient place for baptizing, short of the Ohio River, six miles away.

At one of the evening sessions, when the gospel invitation was extended, a young man, among others, came forward to make the confession. For some reason the doctor doubted his sincerity. So, after taking the confessions of the others, he turned to this young man and asked: "Who

wished you to be baptized?'' He replied : '' Mr.
———.'' '' What did he agree to give you?'' The
answer was : '' Twenty-five cents.'' The person
who hired him to act thus was the son of a
prominent church-member. The incident is a sad
comment on the influence of sectarianism, and a
proof of the truthfulness of the saying that '' our
religion is a persecuting religion.''

During the same meeting another incident occurred which illustrates the wiles of Satan in his
efforts to hinder the progress of truth by making
the ordinances of the gospel of Christ appear
ridiculous.

A man—or one who presented the appearance
of a man—in answer to the inquiry, '' Who is on
the Lord's side?'' came and said that he wished
to do as they did in the days of the apostles (Acts
xvi. 33), be baptized '' the same hour of the
night.'' The doctor, who had seen so many at-
tempts to destroy the effect of his work, was at
once impressed with a conviction that the whole
thing was a scheme of the enemy's. They were
evidently trying to get the preacher and the more
zealous of the church-members to the water, several miles away, that they might find themselves
without a candidate. So, for the first time in his
life, he recommended putting off until to-morrow
what the Lord commanded to be done to-day.
But the Lord also commanded, through Paul, in
First Corinthians iii. 10, that a man should be
careful how he builds on the foundation, which is
Christ. The suspicion proved to be well founded,

for the man, penitent for what he had done, confessed that his only object was to play a trick upon
the preacher.   But the doctor detected the decep-
tion, and he said to the congregation: " If it is a
sheep, it will continue bleating around the fold;
but if a wolf, he will leave when he fails to catch
the prey.''

CHAPTER IX.

AFTER the work closed at Wintersville, Dr. Belding was called to Steubenville to assist in a meeting at that place. Nothing of a very interesting or peculiar character occurred during this time, save one incident, which shows the influence of little things. The doctor had come in contact with some poison vine, and, being very susceptible to its action, was suffering much inconvenience from it; especially about the hands, which were not very presentable for the pulpit. Therefore, to hide their unpleasant appearance, he preached wearing gloves, and that without making an apology or explanation.

Several years had elapsed; when Dr. and Mrs. Belding were once crossing Lake Erie, Mrs. Belding fell in company with an old lady, and they became quite social. It was ascertained that the woman resided in Steubenville, and Mrs. Belding asked her if she had ever attended the Christian Church, or heard their preachers. The reply was: "Not often; but, a number of years since, I heard a young upstart, who preached with his gloves on. That spoiled him for me!" Mrs. Belding called her husband, and, introducing him to the lady, said that she thought he must be the man alluded to, as she had heard him tell the same story.

A revival was in progress at Bellaire, O While Dr. Belding was preaching on New Year's Day, word was brought to the church that the only two

sons of Bro. Archer were drowned in the river.
The whole congregation was thrown into confu-
sion and rushed from the house. A diligent search
was made for the bodies, and they were soon
found, locked in each other's arms. The funeral
was largely attended, and the doctor discoursed
upon the words of the wise man : '' Remember
now thy Creator in the days of thy youth, while
the evil days come not, nor the years draw nigh,
when thou shalt say, I have no pleasure in them ''
(Eccl. xii. 1). Without doubt this dispensation
of affliction had its influence upon the meeting,
since large numbers were gathered into the church.

About the year 1839, in Minerva, Dr. Belding
formed the acquaintance of Charles Louis Loos,
or Charlie Loos, as he was then called. He came
from home to request the doctor's attendance
upon his sister, who was quite ill. From that time
their friendship has been constant and most intimate. When Charlie was quite a boy, Alexander
Wilford Hall and he spent some little time at the
doctor's home. On one occasion Charlie wished
to leave the village quite early in the morning,
and, being more thoughtful than many young men
are, he did not want to disturb the people to get
him an early breakfast. He thought he would
take some bread and milk. But, there being no
bread in the house, he started out to find some.
After calling at the homes of Brethren Whittaker,
Pool and Shrivers, he returned with the sad story
of '' *no bread to be found*,'' remarking that it

would be very difficult, in that village, for a man to live long on bread alone.

Many pleasing incidents are recalled of their intermittent, though almost lifelong, companionship. In later years, Bro. Loos and wife desired to make a visit to New England. They proposed that the doctor accompany them, to which he assented. On their trip, they were permitted to visit nearly all of the Disciples in New England, for they were not numerous. While at Bro. J. C. Talbot's, in East Machias, on the seacoast of Maine, they remained several days without seeing a fish, either on the table or elsewhere. They wondered at it, as they supposed fish would be plentiful there, if anywhere. The doctor asked Sister Talbot if there were no fish in that part of the ocean.

"Fish!" said she; "yes, but we supposed that everybody was tired of fish, just as we are."

"Well," replied the doctor, "*we want fish.*"

"Yes," said Bro. Loos, "fish, *fish*, FISH, FISH, until we say stop."

Here the doctor says: "If you desire a pleasant traveling companion, take the president of Kentucky University with you. You can have fun, anything serious or instructive, as you may desire. He does not think it wicked to laugh, and is in sympathy with the thought that God made this world for men. If kept under the feet, where it belongs, all will be well; but if permitted to get on our heads, it will crush us, or if in our hearts, it will render us miserable forever. The Christian can enjoy all in this world that is worth enjoying, for he has the promise of this life and that which is to come. He who knows us better than we know ourselves has revealed to us his will—a guide to our feet and a lamp to our pathway. Will we walk in the light?''

CHAPTER X.

Dr. Belding was invited by a friend living there to preach a few discourses at Paris, Stark Co., O. But when he arrived, no house could be found in which to speak. The Methodists had the only church building in the place, and, being in power in the community, they closed the schoolhouse against the heretic. But, as often happens, they overshot the mark; for it aroused a feeling, in the non-professing portion of the village, favorable to the heretic. A hotel-keeper came forward and said that he had a ballroom which he would seat and light, and that the doctor might occupy it as long as he pleased. The room was fitted up and crowded with people, curious to hear what the " setters forth of strange doctrine " had to say. The meeting progressed and the interest increased. The people began the cry that " this fellow must be stopped in his work, or he will destroy *our* church and fill the community with his soul-destroying doctrine."

The pastor of the church was approached by anxious members, and urged to interfere and stop the work of the " wolf in sheep's clothing," before he slew the lambs of the fold and scattered the sheep. He was earnestly entreated to enter into a discussion with the doctor, for there was no doubt that the fallacy of the " Campbellite " teaching could easily be shown and its influence annulled. When the pastor was approached by some of the leading members of his church, who

insisted that something *must* be done, he replied:
" I am not going to load a forty-pounder to shoot
a chipmunk."

This, of course, came to the ears of the doctor,
and feeling his spirit stir within him to see the
place wholly given up to Methodism, he without
doubt said some things ,which tended to fan the
flames already existing. At length, the fire became so hot that the pastor began to feel that the
time had come when he ought to escape from the
heat and save the remnant. Now, for the first
time, he consented to hold a debate. Some of
the citizens, not members of the church, came to
the doctor and asked him if he would attempt,
in a public discussion, to defend the position he
had taken. To this he replied : " Yes, and more
also. I will show that the Methodist Discipline
is not only anti-scriptural, but is, in its tendency,
'designed to make infidels instead of Christians."

" What will you discuss? "

" Anything in the Discipline, which is contrary
to the teachings of the Bible."

A number of propositions were submitted, and
agreed upon by both parties. The time and
place for the discussion were fixed, moderators
were chosen, and an anxious community waited
impatiently for the appointed hour. It came, and
with it the crowd of people, for the news had
spread far and wide. When the Methodist Episcopal, " called. and sent," preacher entered the
place for discussion, his arms were loaded with

commentaries. He also had a large pair of old-fashioned "saddle-bags," brought in by an assistant, filled with books. It appeared as if the forty-pounder was loaded, and as though the chipmunk might be in danger. The meeting was opened with prayer. The first proposition for debate was: "Do the Scriptures teach justification by faith only?" Half-hour speeches were agreed upon, and each was to be allowed his full time. "The pastor" arose, and, opening his Bible, read what Paul said upon the subject of justification in Romans and Galatians. When the half-hour was up, the speaker sat down. The doctor arose and stood for a moment in the midst of a deathlike stillness. Picking up the written question from the desk, he read in clear and measured tones: "Do the Scriptures teach justification by faith only?" He then said: "James, we will hear your testimony." Turning to James ii. 24, he read: "You see then how that by *works* a man is justified, and *not by faith only*." Closing the book, he sat down.

The pastor arose for his second half-hour, and occupied it in reading page after page of comments from various authors. "Time expired," called out the moderator. Again Dr. Belding arose to his feet, read the question, and emphasized still more the same answer.

The Methodist pastor, doubtless, felt some annoyance at the turn which the discussion had taken; but he mustered courage to make his

third attempt, which consisted in reading from
manuscript that he had prepared for the occasion.
At the expiration of his time and speech, the
doctor again lifted the paper upon which the
question was written, and said: "Friends and
brethren, this is a *Bible* question, and *must* be
settled by Scriptural authority. Therefore, we
will listen to the declaration of one concerning
whom Jesus said: 'He that heareth you, heareth
me; and he that despiseth you, despiseth me; and
he that despiseth me, despiseth him that sent me.'
James, what is your testimony? 'You see then
how that by *works* a man is justified, and *not by
faith only*' (James ii. 24)." The Methodist
preacher and demolisher of "small animals" did
not wait to discuss the remaining question, but,
in a very excited and angry manner, gathered
up his books, took his hat, and left the house
and congregation.

The only thing left for the doctor to do was
to fill up the time allotted to him, which was one
and a half hours—for he had not used more than
five minutes.

He accordingly delivered a discourse on the
subject of justification, as taught in the Holy
Scriptures. He endeavored to show that *grace
alone* never blessed a man, but simply prepared
the blessing. "*Faith alone*," he asserted, "never
blessed a man, but only led him to *partake* of
the blessing which *grace* had *prepared*. 'For
by grace are ye saved *through faith*,' meaning,

by faith are we led into the grace. By faith we eat and drink, and, in eating and drinking, we are blessed.''

As the visible results of the discussion and preaching, many were brought into Christ and to a knowledge of the truth.

CHAPTER XI.

THE spirit of the doctor was aroused by hearing that a Lutheran minister, by the name of Schafer, near Canton, O., had resolved to expose Campbellism (as he called it) at an appointed time. Word had been widely circulated, as he was a man of some note and would call together many people. Dr. Belding and Alexander Wilford Hall—then a stripling, but afterwards the author of "Universalism Against Itself," and, later, "The Problem of Human Life; or, Evolution Evolved"—determined to hear him.

After riding all day, they reached the place in time to find a large church filled with people. Being strangers, they readily gained admission, and listened to such a harangue and misrepresentation of the Campbellites—or Disciples, as the speaker sometimes called them—as but few men could or would give.

At the close of a lengthy speech, and after the appointments for the next day (Sunday) were given out and the benediction had been pronounced, Dr. Belding asked the attention of the congregation for a few moments. All were seated, and, in breathless silence, wondered what was coming.

The doctor requested the privilege of delivering an address in that house the next morning.

The Rev. Mr. Schafer answered: "We, ourselves, want to use the house."

To this the doctor replied: "We will be through

(44)

with the house before the hour of your service—eleven o'clock." But this met with an emphatic response from the pulpit: "You can not have it, sir."

In reply, the doctor said, in a tone which he intended should be heard by all who were in the house: "Very well, sir; the Lord willing, there will be preaching in the street, opposite this house, to-morrow morning at six o'clock."

The night passed, and, at the appointed hour, a congregation, in number far exceeding what was expected, was in attendance and eager to hear. The place was beautiful—a green plot of grass, shaded by a grove of maples that had been planted to adorn a country churchyard. The services began with the hymn:

"How firm a foundation, ye saints of the Lord,
Is laid for your faith in his excellent word."

Prayer was offered for the divine favor in behalf of the people assembled, and that they might be possessed of the same spirit that Jesus prayed for, as recorded in John xvii. This chapter was read and used as the text of the discourse by Dr. Belding. The *union* of all who believe on Christ, through the teaching of his apostles, was the main topic of the address.

He took the position that to adopt practically the *one creed*—the Bible, which all admit theoretically to be the only infallible guide—and the *one name*—Christian or Disciple of Christ, which is an honor to any one—would result in the bringing together of all who sincerely love Christ, and would thus lead the world to believe that "Jesus is the Christ, the Son of the living God."

The discourse was listened to with attention. At the close, an elderly man stepped forward, and said: "I have a new barn a short distance from here, which I will seat and light. You may preach in it as long as you please."

The doctor asked how soon it could be made in readiness, to which the gentleman answered: "By three o'clock this afternoon." "All right," said the doctor; "there will be preaching, the Lord willing, in the barn this afternoon and evening"

The announcement made and the meeting adjourned, the people gathered in little groups to discuss what they had heard—some favorably impressed, some otherwise. The appointed hour came, and the people were again assembled. After the opening exercises, which were conducted by Dr. Belding, Alexander Hall addressed the audience, taking as a theme, "The Power and All-sufficiency of God's Word in Converting and Saving Men." The train of thought was entirely new to his hearers.

At evening the seats were well filled. The doctor presented the Bible as containing the revealed will of God, and spoke of its power in creation, providence and redemption. After the sermon, he announced that there would be preaching each afternoon and evening, until further notice.

The whole community was aroused, and the

Bible became the general theme of conversation among the people. Meetings continued for some weeks, and scores of people became obedient to the faith. Among them were several members of the Lutheran Church, who had looked in vain for what they had supposed to be clearly taught in the Scriptures, viz. : "infant baptism." When they believed the preaching of Philip concerning the kingdom of God and the name of Jesus Christ, they were baptized, both men and women. (Acts viii.)

Here was organized the first "*Campbellite church*" that has come to our knowledge. Dr. Rufus Belding, father of Dr. W. A. Belding, had defined a Campbellite to be one who believes the doctrine taught by Alexander Campbell, but refuses to obey it. From twenty to twenty-five men, mostly members of the Lutheran Church, formed what *they called* a "Campbellite" church, and appointed their elders and deacons.

The special object of the organization was avowed to be the study of the Scriptures to see whether these things were so. The greater part of them were subsequently baptized, and became members of the church of Christ at Sparta.

Among the number was a young man by the name of Stametts, who, yielding to his convictions of right, after a long study of the Bible, was induced to confess his faith in Christ, and was baptized by Dr. Belding.

This young man's father, one of the leading men in the so-called "Evangelical" church, being very much enraged at the step his son had taken, drove him away from home. Mrs. Stametts (the mother) sent for Dr. Belding to visit her—the doctor thought, professionally. But he found out, on going there, that it was for spiritual, rather than medical, consultation. Father Stametts was so displeased at this that he left the house in a rage.

A few years afterward, Elder Jonas Hartzell went into the neighborhood and delivered a few discourses in the German language. Mr. Stametts, being a German by birth, was induced to hear him, and soon, like thousands of others, fell in love with the simple truth. After a time, he, too, was immersed by Bro. Hartzell.

Dr. Belding, hearing of the change which had taken place, determined to visit Sparta, and call upon the adopted brother. This he did, and, as he was tying his horse to the post, Father Stametts, standing in the door, lifted the glasses from his eyes and discovered the newcomer. He hastened to the gate, crying out: "Vy, Brudder Belding, is dat you! You looks a heap more like a man as you used to do; for you used to look like de werry debil. I always thought de debil and de Campbellite breacher looked zhoost alike."

CHAPTER XII.

At a later meeting held in Sparta, the doctor delivered a discourse upon "The Division of the Word," showing that no new revelations are now made to preachers, but that the injunction to rightly divide the Word of truth is imperative. He then pointed out that the Old Testament contains the account of creation, of the dealings of God with the human family for about sixteen hundred years, of the flood and the repeopling of the earth, together with a further history of the world for twenty-four hundred years until the coming of Christ; that it contains the law, the prophets and the Psalms, and that the special design of it is to point the reader to Christ as the Messiah of God—God's Son and man's only Savior.

He said further that the first four books of the New Testament give an account of the birth, life, death, burial and resurrection of Christ; his commission to the apostles, and his ascension to heaven. The Book of Acts narrates some of the apostles' experiences with sinners, answering the question: "What must I do to be saved?" (See Acts ii. 38; ix. 6; xxii. 16; x. 4, 48; also xvi. 30–33.)

The Epistles were written to believing, penitent, baptized persons; to the individual, the family, the congregation and the church, scattered abroad everywhere. Their design was to teach how to live as Christians and form a Christlike character.

The Book of Revelation describes the Church of Christ, from its organization on the day of Pentecost until the end of time ; telling of past events, others now transpiring, and still others yet to come, closing with a description of the Christian's final home.

When the discourse was ended and the meeting dismissed, an old man, Dr. Tuttle, stepped forward. Taking Dr. Belding by the hand, he said : "My young brother, I have been a preacher in the Methodist Episcopal Church for thirty-six years, and have my license in my pocket But I have learned more about the Bible this evening than in all my life before. Many, many things which have always been mysterious to me have been made plain by the division which you have given us."

After hearing a few discourses, he further said : "I have been a regenerated man for nearly fifty years, but have never been born. I wish to be baptized." His request was granted, and he was immersed in Sandy Creek by Bro. John Whittaker.

To show what prejudice will do, we will further state that his baptism took place Lord's-day morning. In the afternoon of the same day, and at his regular place of preaching, at the close of his sermon, he asked the church for a letter of commendation, saying : "I have my license from the conference, but, wishing to visit the western part of Ohio, I would like a letter, provided you think I am worthy of one." This was freely granted, and a letter given him. But when it was ascertained that he had been immersed, the report was at once circulated that he ought to be excluded from the conference for immoral conduct. He did not wait for the action of that body, but, having been born of water and the Spirit, he took his place among his brethren in Christ, and continued to preach the Word until death called him to lay his armor down.

Soon after this, Dr. Belding moved from Minerva, Stark Co., O., to Doylestown, Wayne County. Here he entered into partnership with Dr. A. L. Simmons, whose wife was a sister to Mrs. Belding, but had recently died. Through the instrumentality of Dr. Belding, a small congregation of Disciples was formed in Doylestown ; so also in Slankertown, two and a half miles away.

To these, as well as other churches, he continued to minister, without money and without price, until it was thought best for him to remove to the latter place. This he did in 1843, boarding for some time with the family of Jacob Huffman, who was an earnest Christian and warm friend.

CHAPTER XIII.

In the small village of Slankertown was a hotel, kept by a German, for whom the village was named. At this place liquors were freely dispensed, which was quite a trial to the doctor, with his strong temperance principles. He repeatedly remonstrated with Mr. Slanker, and tried to persuade him to abandon the sale of intoxicants and keep a temperance house. For a time Mr. Slanker intimated that he would do this. But he at last declared that, if he should give up the sale of whisky, he and his family would starve. The doctor, being somewhat excited, replied: "If you do not keep a temperance house, I will." Upon this they parted, but met again in a few days and resumed the conversation.

The doctor reaffirmed his former statement, and asked Mr. Slanker: "Have you ever known me to lie? My discipline says that I must not lie, and I shall not begin here."

Matters looked very discouraging to a would-be hotel-seeker. He had but a small house; but that was not the greatest obstacle to be overcome. His wife was an invalid, and had not walked a step for many years. But he believed that where there was a will a way could be found. His struggles in earlier life gave him strength and courage, and he at once set about enlarging his house and barn. Within four weeks he put out a sign with this inscription: "Temperance House, by W. A. Belding." This was made so conspicuous that it could be read from one end of the village to the other. The name was familiar, his father having kept a hotel for many years, so he received a steady patronage.

Imagine a man practicing medicine, preaching the gospel, and now, with an invalid and almost helpless wife, attempting to run a hotel. But this he did, and was prospered in all. He finally resolved to dispose of the hotel, abandon the practice of medicine, and devote his life in future exclusively to the proclamation of the gospel of Christ. Ere long an apparent opening presented itself.

During the year 1849, a man who owned a piece of land in Shalersville made a proposal to exchange places with him. The terms were soon arranged, and the contract resulted in the removal of Dr. Belding to the extreme southwest corner of the township of Shalersville. That same year he began preaching for the church at Shalersville Center.

He fitted up two rooms of a dilapidated log house that had come into his possession with the land before mentioned. It was thought that the wife and boy—Rufus E., now about seven years old—could manage to winter there in tolerable comfort. When the family was settled, he commenced a series of meetings in a schoolhouse near by. The interest increased until the house would not hold the audiences.

A lot of wild and reckless boys were in the habit of attending the services, concerning whom

the doctor's nearest neighbor had said, by way
of warning: " You must not leave your carriage,
or anything else which these boys can get hold
of, outside; for they will surely destroy it or
carry it off for you. Indeed, they often take my
carriage wheels and hang them in the tops of
the trees."

The doctor had not forgotten that he was once
young. He accordingly treated the boys kindly,
and in turn found that they were always ready
to do him any favor that he asked.

During the meeting, several converts requested
baptism. The stream was frozen over, but the
boys were on hand. They cleared away the
ice, held the doctor's overcoat and hat, and
helped him into and out of the water, thus showing themselves to be among the warmest friends
he had found in the neighborhood.

The winter passed and the interest was such
in the community about the center of Shalersville that a strong desire was expressed for the
doctor to move into their midst and devote more
time to them. This necessarily involved another
change. Dennis C. Day, a good brother, proposed an exchange of farms with the doctor,
but seven hundred dollars was required by the
doctor to pay the difference in value. How he
should do it and continue preaching was the
question, for he had promised the Lord that he
would continue to preach while he had strength.

Ascertaining by accident that Albert Underwood, the keeper of the poorhouse, was about

to leave that situation, the doctor called on him
and induced him to purchase a half interest in
the new farm for fifteen hundred dollars. Mr.
Underwood worked the farm, while the doctor
preached. But, a year or so afterwards, the
doctor's father, Dr. Rufus Belding, wished to
join his son. The doctor agreed to purchase Mr.
Underwood's half, which his father, in turn,
agreed to buy from him. But after the doctor
had given his notes for Mr. Underwood's interest,
the father suddenly died. How to pay Mr. Underwood fifteen hundred dollars was the question.
However, as usual, a way was found. He sold
the half interest to his brother Edwin, who came
from Randolph, and worked the farm, while the
doctor gave his whole time and attention to the
work of the gospel ministry.

The work of evangelizing seemed to be his
strong point, and nearly one hundred were gathered into the Shalersville Church.

CHAPTER XIV.

In a meeting at which Thomas Munnell was assisting him, a certain young lady made confession of her faith in Christ. While the doctor was consulting with her and arranging for the baptism, the young lady's brother stepped in between his sister and the doctor, declaring that he would shoot any man who attempted to baptize his sister. The doctor very calmly, but decidedly, said to him that if his sister wished to be baptized and desired him to do it, he would undertake it. The brother then said that his sister wished to see her mother, to which the doctor replied: "She can do so if she desires." He asked a young man who stood near to drive his (the doctor's) carriage to the door. The lady and her sister stepped into the carriage, when a *friend* of *her* brother's said that he would drive for them. "Step in and do so," said the doctor. The young man declined, but, upon the doctor's insisting, he finally accepted the invitation and drove off.

By this time the excitement was running high, and some of the people who knew the driver well said to the doctor: "You will not see your horses and carriage again to-night." But he replied that he had no fear of that. They did not return for some time. So Bro. Munnell and the doctor thought it might be well for them to go to the home of the young lady to see what was detaining them. Upon their arrival, they found the young

lady in tears, pleading with her mother for consent, which she positively refused to give.   After
urgent appeals and arguments, she at last yielded.
The doctor took possession of his team, and, with
the young ladies, Bro. Munnell and the young
man who had driven from the church, hastened to
the creek at Bro. Davis Haven's, where the baptism was to be administered.   It was nearly or
quite twelve o'clock, and Bro. Haven's house was
crowded to overflowing.

Some time was spent in prayer, song and exhortation.   Dr. Belding remarked, "There is a
young lady"—pointing towards the sister of the
one about to be baptized — "who told me this
evening, that if it were not for her associates,
she also would confess and obey her Savior,
which she believed to be her duty."

A young man standing near her, after whisper-
ing to her, said: "She says that she never
said so."

The doctor turned to her, and asked : "Harriet,
did you not tell me that this evening?"

"I did," she audibly replied.

Another invitation was 'extended, which four
more accepted, and fourteen were immersed into
Christ without any disturbance whatever.

While living in Shalersville, the doctor spent
a portion of his time in the surrounding towns.
A meeting was appointed in Garrettsville, where
he was expected to preach in the evening   He
drove from his home in the afternoon and stopped
at the house of Bro. Rudolph, who was one of

the elders of the church. As the hour for meeting drew near, it rained in torrents. But Bro.
Rudolph, who was a brave soldier, said: "We
will go to meeting, for we must not let trifles
keep us from the performance of duty." Soon
his carriage was at the door, and his family and
the doctor got into it. The rain increased, and,
just as the elder and the preacher arrived at the
church, the sexton was on the steps, about to
open and light the house. But the sexton said:
"It is useless to open this house to-night, for
no one will be here." Bro. Rudolph turned to
the doctor and asked: "Shall we get out of the
carriage?" The doctor replied: "Do as you
think best, for I will take no responsibility in the
matter." Bro. Rudolph turned his horses and
drove home. On the way they met two men
going to meeting, and in the morning the doctor
met a young lady, who said she was waiting for
the house to be lighted and was intending to go
to church. This caused him to renew a former
pledge, that, if he had an appointment to preach
and had but *one hearer*, he would preach to
that one.

Only a few weeks had elapsed when he went
to Streetsboro to fill an engagement in a schoolhouse. Upon entering, he found it empty. He
took his Bible, and, while he was reading, three
men came in. Two of them he knew to be members of the church, while one was not. The rain
was falling copiously, and one of the brethren
proposed that they all go across the street to hear

what the Báptist minister might have to say. The doctor said that if they would remain, he would preach to them. They assented, and he addressed the two brethren for perhaps thirty minutes. He then turned and spoke to the man of the world, closing with a personal appeal: "Do you believe what I have said?" He replied: "I do." "Do you intend ever to become a Christian?" He answered promptly: "I do." The question was then put, "When?" and as promptly answered: "I will start to-day." The confession of his faith in Christ was then taken, and the preacher and congregation repaired to the stream, where he was buried in the baptismal grave, arising to walk in "newness of life." He has often since been heard to say: "If the house had been full, I would, doubtless, have gone as I came; but, the preaching being personal, I could not resist it."

Dr. Belding was engaged in a meeting in Ravenna, O., when, in response to the gospel invitation, a lady confessed her faith in Christ. Her husband left the house in a rage. When the wife returned to her home, he met her at the door, and, in a most profane and abusive manner, forbade her going to the church again. On Mon day morning he was so angry that he left home for his school (he was a teacher) without his breakfast. His wife was very unhappy until Wednesday, near the middle of the day, when, on looking out the window, she saw him coming home. On arriving at the house, he asked her to come to the door where he had met her on that previous evening. Making an humble apology, he asked her to forgive him, saying that if she would go with him, he, too, would confess his Savior. This he did, and they were forthwith baptized.

It is better sometimes to move people even to anger than to have them remain in a state of indifference. Many cases bear witness to this.

While an invitation hymn was being sung at Pompey Hill, N. Y., the leader of the music being an unbeliever, the doctor asked that the singing cease for a moment. He inquired if there were not persons in the room who were singing sentiments that they did not believe. The leader, Mr. Ellis, threw aown his book, took his hat and left the house, looking mad enough to fight. He told his wife that he would never enter the church again.

Two years or more passed. The doctor was holding a meeting at Cato, Cayuga Co., N. Y. Mrs. Ellis, of Pompey, came into the house. At the close of the services, the doctor inquired after the welfare of herself and family. She burst into tears, and, after she had controlled her feelings sufficiently, related to him the story concerning her husband, as above stated. The doctor, who was accustomed to looking on the bright side of the picture, said: "Do not grieve, for I intend going to Pompey when this meeting is over."

The time came, and the meeting in Pompey was in progress. Mr. Ellis brought his family to church and took them home.   As the people were getting into their carriages after service, the doctor heard Mr. Ellis asking Bro. Joseph Garrett and wife to go home to dine with them.   The doctor said to himself: "Now is my time." Stepping up to Mrs. Ellis, he said: "I think I will take dinner with you to-day."   She responded: "I wish you would."   Dr. Belding stepped into the carriage with Bro. Garrett's people, and they arrived at the house a little in advance of the family.   When Mr. Ellis drove up, the doctor, in a very jovial manner, came forward, and, reaching out his hand, said: "How do you do, Bro. Ellis?"

Mr. Ellis extended his hand rather reluctantly, and, in a reserved manner, said: "How are you?"   The doctor continued: "I don't know that you can put up with such fare as we have here, but we would like to have you come in and take some dinner with us."   "All right," said Mr. Ellis.   The doctor went to the barn, assisted in putting up the horses, looked over the farm, went to the house and took dinner.   After a good social time, as the hour for evening meeting drew nigh, he said to Mr. Ellis: "Come, hitch up that nice team and take us to church.   We can not afford to walk with such good horses standing idle."   To this he readily consented.   The doctor sat beside him on the way to church, and said: "Hitch your horses under the shed and go to meeting with us."   He made no reply, but the doctor repeated the invitation more earnestly, when Mr. Ellis reluctantly said: "I will think of it." The friends alighted and entered the house. Presently, to the astonishment of all, Mr. Ellis came in. The next evening found him in attendance, and the third day witnessed what his friends had long desired, but had never dared hope for — the confession of his confidence in Christ.

After his baptism and change of raiment, the doctor addressed him: " Well, Bro. Robert, how do you feel?" His answer was: " I feel good, and not much as I did two years ago, when I angrily left the church." He added: " Now I am thankful for the merited rebuke. It was *that* which saved me."

Another incident of a similar nature occurred in Chardon, Geauga Co., O. An interesting meeting was in progress. The congregation was singing the hymn of invitation, when, suddenly, the doctor called out, " Please stop singing," and asked: " Which is the worse—to *tell* a falsehood or to *sing* it?" One of the leading singers, a daughter of the resident pastor, drew her veil over her face, stepped across the aisle, and dropped into her seat. With a deep sigh the pastor, Bro. Collins, exclaimed: " Oh, dear!" Bro. Collins and the doctor were singing from the same book. The doctor replied: " Bro. Collins, don't be alarmed, for I think I know Lizzie well, and I do not believe I have missed the mark." He was right, for in a day or two Lizzie was obedient to her Savior.

CHAPTER XV.

DURING the years of Dr. Belding's stay in Shalersville, he was called to fill an appointment of Calvin Smith's in Austintown, O., from which Bro Smith was detained by sickness. The meeting had continued but a short time when the brethren of the church came, and, in great distress, begged of the doctor that he would give no invitation for "backsliders" to return to the church. They feared that a man, who in former years had been excluded from the church for his continued litigation and contention with a fellow-townsman, might ask for admission. The two men could never meet without exchanging angry words, and two or three times had come to blows. All felt certain that, if he returned, the church must have trouble with him, and would, no doubt, be again compelled to withdraw the hand of fellowship from him.

He and his avowed enemy were in the house at every service, but as far removed from each other as they well could be. The doctor, who declares that by nature he is cowardly, studied carefully to avoid all suggestions that might be construed into an invitation for the wanderer to return to the fold, and really failed to do his duty. Upon one occasion, when speaking of the power of the gospel to make the warmest friends of bitterest enemies—able even to turn "a raven to a dove, a lion to a lamb"—he mustered up courage, after breathing an earnest prayer for help, to do his duty. He asked: "Are there not several present who have known the joy arising from the assurance of sins forgiven by obedience to Christ, and the hope of eternal life—who have wandered from their Father's house and feel like returning? If so, let them come." No sooner was the opportunity offered than the wanderer came to the front. At the same moment the other man appeared, coming from the opposite side of the house. Consternation filled the hearts of the congregation, and especially that of the doctor, who felt that a collision was inevitable, and that the contentious parties would break up the meeting with an excited row. But great was the relief when the two men, who for many years had been at swords' points, met as friends, throwing their arms around each other, and, each with his head resting on the other's shoulder, with tears of penitence confessed his faults, each asking the forgiveness of the other, of the congregation, and of God.

This was one of the most touching scenes of the kind that Dr. Belding has ever witnessed, and one of the most convincing evidences of the power of the gospel of Christ over the hearts and lives of men.

"How sweet the name of Jesus sounds
    In a believer's ear;
It soothes his sorrows, heals his wounds,
    And drives away his fear.

"It makes the wounded spirit whole,
    And calms the troubled breast;
'Tis manna to the hungry soul,
    And to the weary rest."

CHAPTER XVI.

On the twentieth day of August, 1855, in company with his brother Edwin and two friends, Harmon Lake and Wallace Hunt (the latter of Auburn, N. Y.), the doctor left home for the West. The boys, Edwin and his companions, had with them ten horses, which they designed selling in Chicago, if not successful in disposing of them before reaching that place. Mrs. Belding accompanied the doctor, but was to leave the party at the then celebrated "water cure" at Berlin, O. On the second day, towards evening, the party arrived at Berlin, where Mrs. Belding remained, while the rest of the party pushed on. During the third day the doctor traded his black team for a gold watch, and traveled with the rest of his party to Maumee City, where they paused to inspect old Fort Meigs. They found some relics of battle, among which were several human teeth. Hastily leaving Maumee City, where over half of the people were sick—it being a very unhealthy place—they advanced, stopping occasionally to call on an acquaintance. The doctor preached nearly every evening.

They passed through Hillsdale, Coldwater, Bronson, White Pigeon and Elkhart, to South Bend, Ind., which they reached on the 31st of August. The 4th of September found them in Chicago This was the doctor's first sight of that now tremendous and unrivaled city, and he described it as "no city at all; very rough,

(65)

uneven, unpaved, a malarial place of a few thousand people, and in no way attractive or promising.''

A sister in Austintown, O., after supporting herself and an invalid mother for a number of years by her needle, left fifty-one dollars and a few cents in the hands of Brethren Joseph Karl and Joseph Kyle, with the request that they should use it to the best of their judgment to pay for preaching the gospel. Dr. Belding went to a place near New Castle, Pa., called Pumpkintown, where he preached ten days, and was paid one dollar per day from this fund.

He has said that he scarcely ever felt the inspiration to preach that he felt there, as if a voice from the grave was constantly urging him to make known to his fellowmen the wondrous love of God. Three other churches were then brought into existence by that small, but liberal, donation.

The year 1855 was spent almost entirely in holding meetings and soliciting funds for the General Missionary Convention. A meeting held by the doctor at South Butler, N. Y., resulted in the immersion of sixty-seven persons.

From South Butler he went to New York City, where he remained but a few days, immersing nineteen. We find him next at Danbury, Conn., tarrying at the home of Bro. E. A. Mallory (a long-tried friend), and holding a meeting in the Danbury Church. The result of this effort was the adding of between fifty and sixty to the membership.

The last evening of the meeting, after closing the church and upon returning home in company with Bro. Mallory and wife, they found awaiting them two young ladies, employes of Bro. Mallory. They had been steadily attending the meetings, and were now crying and sobbing because the meeting was past, and they had not found courage to confess their belief in Christ. A service was held then and there, for their dear sakes, in which they confessed their Savior, and stated their desire to be immersed. It was then between twelve and one o'clock at night, and the doctor was to leave the town early in the morning. Arousing a few of the brethren who lived near by, the party started for a neighboring stream. Before they had gone many rods, a large distillery began to burn fiercely, and afforded them ample light for the ceremony.

During all this time his home was in Shalerville. But, in 1856, he sold his remaining interest in the farm to a brother-in-law of Edwin's, Elwood Hamilton, and moved to Mentor, Lake Co., O., early in 1857.

At a yearly meeting held in Randolph, Portage County, in June, 1852, he had the pleasure of baptizing Rufus E., at that time his only son, aged eleven years, in the stream in which he was himself immersed some years before.

CHAPTER XVII.

Soon after moving to Mentor, the doctor bought a place of about ten acres in the center of the township, and within sight of the Garfield residence, which has since made Mentor known to the nation. While engaged in holding a meeting at Bedford, O., soon after he had moved his family to Mentor, an incident occurred. During the singing of a song of invitation, Dr. J. P. Robinson, who was extremely anxious for the salvation of his only sister, approached her, and kindly said: "Come, go with us, and we will do you good." She shook her head, and he returned to his place near the pulpit. Not feeling satisfied, he went to her again, but with the same result. Still the brother could not feel content, and returned the third time, *pleading* with her to yield to the invitation of the loving Savior, but again she refused. The meeting closed, and, soon after, the young lady was taken suddenly ill, and drew rapidly near the end of life. Calling her brother to her bedside, she said: "You came to me once, twice, three times, and urged me to confess my faith in Christ, and I as stubbornly refused your loving opportunity. *Why did you not come again?* I meant in my heart to yield, but you did not come, and I was left—yes, left to die without hope." "Go into the highways and hedges, and compel them to come in," said our blessed Savior.

Being called to Bainbridge, O., to spend a few days, he was invited to preach in the Congregational Church. The invitation was accepted. During the series of discourses which he gave, there was one of his hearers—a lady from New York—who became deeply impressed with the truth of what she heard. She sent the doctor a note, asking him to call on her, expressing a desire to converse with him privately. He promptly complied with her request, and found her an intelligent and conscientious woman, a member of the M. E. Church. She said she was troubled about her baptism, concerning which she had never had a doubt until she heard the few discourses delivered by him, one of which was a discussion of the subject, "A Penitent Believer."

After asking a number of questions, which were answered to her satisfaction, she asked if he would baptize her, and allow her to retain her membership in the M. E. Church, and added: "There is no other where I live, and I do not know as I would join one if there was." To this question the doctor answered: "I will baptize you with the understanding that you will follow the teaching of the Lord Jesus Christ and the apostles. If they make of you a Methodist, *be one;* if a Presbyterian, *be one;* if a Baptist, or even a Mormon, *be one.* In short, *go* where the Bible leads you, and *be* what the Bible makes you." To this the lady replied: "I resolved many years ago to do all the Savior asks of me as fast as I can learn my duty." Upon a confession of her faith in Christ she was immersed.

A few weeks later the doctor was called to

attend a funeral in the same town. The lady was present, and at the close of the services she approached the doctor, requesting a letter or certificate of her baptism, at the same time stating that she was going to spend the winter in Cincinnati, and would like to spend it with the " Church of Christ." The doctor said, smilingly : " You will doubtless find a Methodist church there also." She quickly responded : " I have learned *too much* to be a Methodist, and prefer to be simply and only a Christian." The letter was, of course, granted.

The saying of Him who spake as never man spake, " Except a man love me more than all else, he can not be my disciple," is sometimes put to the test. A single instance will illustrate. Dr. Belding was called to attend the funeral of one whom he supposed to be a stranger. But, upon entering the house and looking upon the face of the sleeper, he at once recognized it as a familiar one, and one having a sad, but interesting, history.

· Many years before, while Bro. William Hayden was preaching at Royalton, O., a young lady was most forcibly impressed with his clear and touching presentation of the simple " story of the cross." Her father was an infidel, while the mother and all the members of her family were scoffers at the Christian religion ; nevertheless, her interest increased and her convictions deepened. Her father told her emphatically that if she joined that despised little company, she could no longer have a home with him.

After calm and serious reflection, and most earnest prayer, she decided to follow Christ. She was immersed by Bro. Hayden, and went from the stream to her father's home, only to be denied admittance. She turned away, and though for eighteen long years she lived within ten miles of her childhood home, yet she spoke to but one member of her family, and never was allowed to enter the old home, during that time. None of her relatives were present at her funeral—to see her carried to her resting-place. Her closing hour was peaceful, and when her eyes were growing dim with death's approach, she said to those around her : ". I am going to see the loving Savior, for whom I have forsaken all." Jesus verified to her his promise here, and will no doubt do so as fully in the new Jerusalem. " *He is truthful*," " *he is faithful;* " " he gives homes and friends an hundred-fold."

CHAPTER XVIII.

In 1849, during the annual meeting being held at Russell, Geauga Co., O., a few brethren were called together in the house of Bro Lattin Soule to consult with reference to the propriety of building a school for the education of their children—not only in the sciences, but also in the Bible. We will give the doctor's connection with this work in his own language.

" I was present at that meeting, and when the plan was agreed upon and the determination made to go ahead with the work, I was selected as its financial and general agent. The raising of the sum needed for such an enterprise seemed like a great undertaking for a people so weak financially and so few in numbers. But I succeeded in raising the first twenty-five thousand dollars contributed to lay the foundation of the Western Reserve Eclectic Institute, which has since grown into the well-known and reputable educational institution called Hiram College.

" I am now (1897) the only person living who was present at that preliminary meeting. I naturally feel proud of the work there inaugurated and so prosperously carried on. God's blessing has attended it from the first, and many noble men and women have gone forth from its halls who have honored the institution, and aided to fill the world with the knowledge and spirit there impressed upon them. Among those best known to the American people was James A. Garfield, a graduate from, and afterwards the president of,. the college. May it long continue to prosper,. and when those who so generously contributed to its support shall be gathered to their fathers,. and rest from their labors, may their work still continue, that future generations may call them: blessed."

In this work, and in his labor for the missionary society of Ohio, he gained the reputation of being a "*successful beggar*," as he himself has. expressed it.

While engaged in these works, he often found persons who expressed the wish to donate to the object for which he was soliciting, but who plead the excuse that they had no money ; but if they could sell such a piece of property—a horse, a cow or a piece of land—they *would do so*.

The doctor was always ready for such emergencies, and would propose to take the property and pay to the institute its value. Upon one occasion, he visited a man from whom, it was said, nothing could be [obtained. In the midst of harvest, when work was pressing hard, the doctor called early in the morning and found the family at breakfast with a number of hired men. Being invited, he took breakfast with them. When, rising from the table, the brother remarked, "You must excuse me, for my work is pressing," he replied : "The Master's work is always pressing, and I am in a hurry, too." He made known the object of his visit, and asked for the modest sum of one hundred dollars. To

this request the miserly brother replied quickly
and rather excitedly, "I am so much in debt
that I can not give you one hundred cents," and
he started for the harvest field.   The doctor called
him back, and kindly entreated him to give him
a promise for the amount, but he insisted that he
could not afford it.

The doctor knew that, like many others, before
he had one farm paid for he would buy another,
keeping always in debt, and thus always having
that as an excuse for not giving.   He finally sat
down, and, in the course of the conversation that
ensued, told the doctor what liabilities he had
outstanding.   After much persuasion, he gave his
note for the amount asked for, due one year after
his last obligation was due.   This he did as much
to get rid of his visitor as from any other motive.
It was collected from his estate, as he died before
it became due.   The doctor's comment on the
above, as found in his diary, is slightly humorous.
It stands: "The Lord loveth the cheerful giver."

CHAPTER XIX.

In 1856, Bro. Garrett, of Pompey, N. Y., had a little money, which he desired to devote to the Master's cause. Fifty dollars of this money he handed to the doctor to assist some young man in preparing for the ministry. After keeping it for some time without finding a place where it seemed needed, he at length gave to C. C. Foote fifteen dollars, with which to buy an overcoat. Soon after, the doctor wrote Bro. Garrett that he had thirty-five dollars in his pocket, and asked what disposition he desired made of that amount. To this Bro. Garrett replied: "Go and preach it out."

The place selected was Wellington, a town in Ohio, between Cleveland and Columbus. After repeated efforts to obtain a house to preach in, a certain Mr. Tripp (a man of the world) came to the doctor and said: "I have a carriage shop, which I will heat and light; there you can preach as long as you wish." The invitation was accepted and the meeting began. The novelty of the place attracted the people, and from the first the attendance was good. Converts were made, and soon a congregation was formed amid much sectarian prejudice and opposition, which became so manifest that the sympathies of "outsiders" were aroused, and a subscription was started. Soon the building of a house of worship was commenced and ultimately finished, owing largely to the assistance rendered by non-professing citizens.

(75)

When Bro. Garrett was informed of what had been accomplished, he said: "Thank God! I have fifty dollars more to spend in the same way."

During the same year Dr. Belding was preaching at Madison, Lake Co., O., when an invitation was given him to speak in the Presbyterian Church upon the subject, "Christian Union." This he consented to do on the following Lord's-day evening. The house was crowded, and the congregation so much interested and pleased with the manner in which the subject was presented that one of the officers in the church arose and asked the speaker if he would not speak to them again. The doctor replied that he would be pleased to do so, providing he was assured that his hands should not be tied, nor his tongue padlocked. The man who made the request rose again to his feet, and responded: "We would like to have you preach here every evening until we request you to stop." He called upon three others of the trustees, all of whom expressed themselves in favor of continuing the meeting. The pastor of the church objected in quite a spirited speech, but the trustees prevailed, and the meeting went on.

A number of persons declared that they had learned the way of the Lord more perfectly, and were determined to walk in it. They were baptized into Christ, ignoring their former " baptism" while unbelieving infants.

CHAPTER XX.

THE meeting at South Butler, N. Y., to which reference has been made, had in it several items of interest. A number of invitations had been given the doctor to visit that congregation, each of which he refused without giving any reason for the refusal. A committee was finally sent to Auburn. They succeeded in getting his consent to assist them in a meeting when his labors were ended in Auburn.

The time arrived, and he was on hand. The first week the time was spent in trying to arouse the spirituality of the church, which was at a very low ebb. On Saturday afternoon, while one of the elders was speaking, another spoke out excitedly: "If you believe *that*, you don't believe the Bible."

When he sat down the doctor arose and said: "This gives me a good opportunity to say what I have had on my mind ever since I came here. The reason I refused to come here was that I had heard of you as a congregation of intelligent Disciples, *full of discussion* and possessing very little spirituality. And what have you accomplished? It is evident that you have a good knowledge of the *letter* of the *law* of Christ, but have failed to catch the spirit of its author, and by your oft-repeated discussions have driven away (if you ever had it) the Spirit of the Master. You have failed to observe the injunction of Paul, 'Speak the truth in love,' until you are driving

(77)

your own children and your neighbors' children
out of the church. Let us see! Bro. Lowell,
your pastor, has not a member of his family, save
himself and wife, in the church. It has often
been said to me: 'Elder Lowell is a man of
splendid talent, but no religion.' Elders Dratt
and Johnson have children who should have become members long ago. The members of Elder
Laing's [another preacher] household are in the
same condition. Brethren, you are not blind and
can see this. Bro. Lowell has done *one part*
of his work well, in fulfilling the old saying:
'Like priest, like people.' He has filled them
with the spirit of 'dispute.'"

Bro. Lowell was sitting by and weeping like a
child. When the opportunity occurred, he arose
and said: "I have always supposed it was our
duty to contend earnestly for the faith once delivered to the saints, but I see now that the
manner in which I have done so has been wrong."
He was followed by a number of others, who,
like their pastor, confessed that they had been
wrong when they supposed they were right. Such
a breaking down of spirit is not often witnessed.
On the last morning of the meeting, twenty-two
were baptized — among them Dr. Sweeting, a
Methodist class leader. In all, sixty-seven were
added to the church, and the vitality of the congregation was greatly improved.

A number of years later, the doctor assisted in
holding another meeting at South Butler, where
he baptized one hundred and sixty-seven persons.

During this meeting, he was called upon to attend the funeral of a young Bro. Hibbard, who was a devoted Christian and a teacher in the Sunday-school. After the funeral services and during the Sunday-school, the doctor was called upon to make a few remarks. During a short speech, he suggested that there were at least one hundred young persons in that school who ought to confess their Savior. This thought stimulated the brethren and the doctor. The meeting was continued,. and, in less than three weeks, the one hundred spoken of were added to the church. Among those added was a beautiful girl of thirteen, the youngest among the new converts and an only child. She was of an affectionate disposition. At the social meeting, in which a great number took part, she said that for many days she had desired to obey her Savior, but she had wanted papa and mamma to go with her. As they would not, she had gone alone. But, turning toward her father and mother, who were present, she said: " How I wish that they would now accept Christ as their Savior, and be as happy as I am." They both arose, and she led them forward, amid the common rejoicing and tears. "And a little child shall lead them."

At the close of the meeting in South Butler,. the doctor was invited by a Congregational minister to go to Savannah (four miles distant) to help hold a meeting. The doctor was inclined to accept the invitation, but did not feel like compromising in any way the truth of our plea. He insisted that he should be allowed perfect freedom to speak the truth, as he understood it, from God's word. "That," said the preacher, "is what I want you to do." Accordingly, the meeting was commenced at once. The congregation grew in numbers and the interest increased, until sinners began to inquire, "What shall we do to be saved?" The doctor, turning to the preacher, who was sitting beside him in the pulpit, said: "Bro. P——, what shall I tell these convicted inquirers?" Bro. P——, himself apparently deeply moved, said: "Bro. Belding, did I not tell you to preach the truth?" "Yes." "Well, then do so." The doctor thereupon gave them the same answer that Peter gave to the people on Pentecost (Acts ii. 38): "Repent, and be baptized every one of you in the name of Jesus Christ for the remission of sins, and ye shall receive the gift of the Holy Spirit. For the promise is unto you, and to your children, and to all that are afar off, even as many as the Lord our God shall call."

In response to an invitation which followed, a number of the old members of the church responded, and, encouraged by their pastor *to live up to their convictions*, they were immersed into Christ Jesus. At the close of his labors, the pastor arose, and, in a very feeling manner, said: "I am sorry Dr. Belding is to leave us, for I have been deeply interested, encouraged and in-

structed.'' After the meeting closed, and they
had retired to the pastor's study, the doctor said :
'' Bro. P——, *I* am sorry that I am going to
leave, for I would like to stay long enough to
baptize you and the rest of your congregation.''
'' That you would do,'' responded Bro. P——,
'' if all doubts on the subject were removed.''

A few months after this pleasant interview, Mr.
P—— was called very suddenly from his labors—
falling dead in his pulpit on a Lord's-day morning.

CHAPTER XXI.

MRS. BELDING was an invalid almost from the time of her marriage. The first eighteen months of their married life she was sick, and, though better at times, was unable to walk a step for fourteen years. During nine years of this time, the doctor used a crutch or a cane to assist his own steps; but he finally recovered the use of his limb, although ever since compelled to wear an elastic stocking.

His beloved wife, of whom he took the most tender care, finally died of nervous fever, at Mentor, O., November 25, 1860. The following extracts from the doctor's diary for 1860 speak with a pathos that shows the strong affection of the man for his family:

Sept. 29.—But little sleep; Myra sick all night,

Oct. 1.—Still very sick. I was confined at home all day.

Oct. 5.—A little better; Rufus at home.

Oct. 11.—Myra no better that I can see. Drs. Rosa and Stebbins say that she is doing well, but I do not believe it.

Oct. 18.—At home all day. Dr. Rosa here; Myra no better.

Nov. 1.—Myra no better; sick five weeks to-day.

Nov. 3.—Myra failing; Rufus at home.

Nov. 7.—Meeting of the Missionary Board at Bedford. Could not leave Myra to attend. Went to bed the first time in six weeks.

Nov. 8.—Sent Rufus to Painesville for Dr. Stockton.

(82)

Nov. 12.—Myra no better. Bro. A. S. Hayden and wife came to see us, and spent the night.

Nov. 13.—Myra had a very sick day.

Nov. 15.—Myra very sick and vomiting. Sister Lucy Clapp and Mrs. Shoemaker took care of her all night. I have taken care of her, until this time, for seven weeks. Dr. Stebbins and Dr. Storm came to see her to-day. They say that she must starve to death. (Terrible to think of!)

Nov. 17.—Myra failing; suffering beyond anything I ever witnessed. Her mind as clear as a cloudless sky. Happy in the love of God and the bright hope of heaven. Says: "Tell all my friends that my feet are on the Rock."

Nov. 18.—Myra but just alive. Twice this morning she requested me to go and preach to the people, saying: "Give them my dying love; tell them to examine well the ground of their hope. I am happy, for I am almost home." A very hard day for me.

Nov. 19.—Myra very low. A number of calls to see her.

Nov. 23.—Myra very low. It does not seem as though she could stay another day. Suffering much, but calm and very quiet.

Nov. 24.—Myra had a very sick night; talked much; had not a doubt as to her future bliss. Bade us good-by; had a sinking turn, but revived. Could not talk plainly; was much distressed for breath.

Nov. 25.—At home by the bedside of our dear
Myra, until she died at 10:45 A.M. Felt a
calmness and quiet when she breathed her last
that I had not felt for weeks during her suffering, which was most severe.

Nov. 27.—Funeral at 1 P.M. Bro. A. S. Hayden
preached, by request, from 1 Cor. xv. and 2
Cor. v. Selected hymns: "Rock of Ages,"
"Why Should We Mourn?" "Departed
Friends," and "Asleep in Jesus."

The following obituary was written by a lifelong friend:

"Died, on Lord's-day, the 25th of November,
1860, of nervous fever, Mrs. Myra E. Belding,
consort of Dr. W. A. Belding, of Mentor, O.;
aged 47 years, 1 month and 22 days.

"Long and gradual has been her descent of
the hill of life. For a period of twenty-four years
she has been the subject of severe afflictions, and
some fourteen years of that time she was so extremely feeble as not to be able to walk or to
stand on her feet. Much of the time, so extreme
was her frailty that cradled innocence was scarcely
more helpless. Yet no murmur escaped her
uncomplaining lips. Remarkably patient and
hopeful throughout her protracted debility, she
manifested a resignation, and even cheerfulness,
that commanded the admiration of all who enjoyed
an acquaintance with her. No pain or depression
from an illness so tedious and discouraging ever

disturbed for an hour the equanimity of her feelings—as balmy and genial as a morning in May.
Having chosen in early life the Savior as her
portion and her hope, she maintained a highly
consistent profession of the gospel, which shed
the radiance of its brightest hopes over her spirit
as she verged on the confines of eternity.

"Along with her calmness of spirit there was
associated a Christian benevolence untiring in its
assiduities for the welfare of all around her.
Often, when so feeble as to be unable to lift her
head from her pillow, she urged her husband ·to
fill his appointments, willing to suffer any priva-
tion that the salvation of the people might be
promoted. Even the last Lord's-day of her stay
on earth she said to him: 'Go .to your appointment to-day; you may be the means of saving
some poor sinner. Give the church my dying
message of love. Exhort all to look well to the
ground of their hope, and tell them I am happy;
that my feet are on the rock. The Lord will
sustain me till you return.'

"She grieved lest she might ever have said
anything to discourage him in the work of carrying the gospel to the dying world.

"As might be expected from such a spirit and
such a life, her last sickness, of two months' con-
tinuance, was crowded with evidences, which
grew brighter and more frequent to its close, of
a most peaceful and even exultant departure to
the rest that remains for the people of God."

(Signed) A. S. HAYDEN.

CHAPTER XXII.

THE work of establishing a nucleus in Syracuse and erecting a church is told in the doctor's own language. The writer simply verified the dates from diaries, covering the years during which he labored there.

" In the fall of 1862, while residing at Mentor, O., I received a letter from Sister Wealthy Ann Allen, of Auburn, N. Y., asking me to visit her, at her expense, in the interest of the Master's cause.

" I accepted the invitation, and arranged to comply at once with her request. The facts, as related by Sister Allen and as recorded in my diary, are these :

" In her girlhood days, while she was engaged in teaching in the then small city of Syracuse, she picked up a leaf or two of a monthly pamphlet, which she afterward learned was called the ' Millennial Harbinger.' Upon these torn and dirty leaves she found a sentiment expressed which arrested her attention, and in a manner that led her to take it to her pastor for an explanation.

" After looking at it for a moment, he said, with much earnestness : ' That is rank Campbellism, and will ruin you, soul and body, for time and for eternity. Have nothing to do with it.'

" She found out by him where and by whom it was published, and wrote for it the same day. In about eighteen months she was asked to renounce

the sentiment imbibed, or submit to an exclusion
from the fellowship of the church on the charge
of heresy. She preferred the latter, for the reason that her convictions would not permit her to
accept the former. Accordingly, she was excluded. She then and there resolved that if
spared, and if the Lord permitted means to come
into her possession, the primitive gospel should
be preached in Syracuse.

" She further informed me that an uncle of
hers, now deceased, had left her seven hundred
dollars. Three hundred of this she gave me,
wishing me to hire a hall and begin work at
once.

" This I did, and January 21, 1863, I preached
my first discourse in the City Hall. After thoroughly advertising, we succeeded in getting
together fourteen hearers, but I find recorded in
my diary, in addition to the above, the following :

Jan. 24.—The beginning is small, but the Lord's
    blessing upon our labors will cause it to be suc-
    cessful. We hope to continue until the truth
    shall win its way, and the Church of Christ
    be firmly established here.

Jan. 24.—Preached three times in the City Hall
    to-day. Interest increasing, and the opposition
    also. Twice the number that were present one
    week ago.

Jan. 30.—Great reason for encouragement in at-
    tendance and interest.

" A number of persons wishing to be immersed,
I asked for the use of a baptistery belonging to a

certain religious body in the city. They called together the Board of Trustees, and, after a full and free discussion of the subject, passed the following resolutions, to-wit:

" 'Whereas, Dr. Belding has asked for the use of our baptistery, in which to baptize some converts, we feel compelled to refuse him for this reason: the nearer a counterfeit is to the genuine, the more dangerous.'

" A Dr. Ray came to me at once, and asked if I had been refused the use of the baptistery. I replied in the affirmative. He then said: ' I have a large number of dressing-rooms attached to my bathing-park, and, although I belong to the big church, I like fair play. You are welcome to the use of as many of those rooms as you wish, and as often as you wish. They will be warmed for you free of charge.' We accepted his kind and generous invitation, and used it many times until we had a baptistery of our own.

" The papers several times refused to publish notices of our meetings. At length I was so much annoyed by them that I wrote a request for one of the editors, as follows: ' The prayers of this union meeting are most earnestly requested for the editor of one of our daily papers—that his heart may be opened, so that he will consent to publish the religious notices of a feeble church, which is trying to honor God and bless the world.'

" With this notice in my pocket, I started for the meeting, with a firm resolution to present it.

But, meeting one of the local editors, I read him the request, and told him my determination. He begged of me not to do it, and said that anything I wished published, if I would bring it to him, should be done. From that time we had no further trouble.

Feb. 8.—I preached in the morning, and, after baptizing nine persons upon a profession of their faith in Christ, we took the preliminary steps toward an organization. Thirty-five persons who had given themselves to the Lord now pledged themselves one to another to accept the teachings of Christ and the apostles as their guide of life, discarding all humanly formulated creeds and man-given titles. Sister Allen, from Auburn, being present with us, spoke many pleasant and encouraging words, and closed by saying, in a very feeling manner: ' It is the happiest day of my life. Now, Lord, let thou thy servant depart in peace, for I have seen thy salvation.'

" She then pledged two hundred dollars towards the erection of the building in which we are gathered this evening, and which was the first subscription made.

Feb. 15.—Preached twice. Received nine into the fellowship of the church and baptized two. Hall well filled, with a good representation from the religious community and the world.

May 10.—Baptized three. The interest not abated in the least.

Nov. 22.—We meet to-day for the first time in
the Courthouse, and are much pleased with the
change from the City Hall.   Things are looking
hopeful, and yet the papers refuse us a fair
representation, even when paid for publishing
notices of our meetings and work.

" From this time until June 17, we continued
to meet in the Courthouse, with a fair attendance
and , frequent additions.   On June 19, 1864, the
new church building was formally opened, Bro.
D. S. Burnett preaching a very appropriate dedi-
catory discourse   In the evening services were
held, and three persons confessed their faith in
Christ.

June 19.—Met on this the first Lord's-day in the
new church building.   Bro. Burnett preached,
and I baptized eight persons, making eighteen
since the opening of the house.

June 25.—Meeting again this evening ; three bap-
tisms and four other confessions.

June 26.—Closed the meeting this evening, with
thirty-one added to the church.

July 3.—Several added to the church to-day.
Organized a Sunday-school and Bible class,
with about thirty in each.

Aug. 28, 1864.—This closes my engagement in
this church, which was organized with thirty-
five members, and now numbers one hundred
and three.   A house has been built costing
fifteen thousand dollars, of which twelve thousand are paid.

" I continued my work with the congregation until some time in 1865, when I resigned my position, and was followed by Bro. A. N. Gilbert, the membership having increased to one hundred and twenty-eight. My labors closed with the consciousness that I never had a more earnest and faithful company of helpers than I left in Syracuse. I parted from them with strong attachments.

" The resolutions passed and the presents received have been kept, and the memory of them cherished most tenderly, even to this day. They will be a source of comfort to myself and family while memory retains its sway. I might speak with tender feeling and deepest emotion of individual co-laborers, some of whom still linger, while others are on the other shore, awaiting the reunion of the family in the mansions prepared by the Elder Brother, where there will be no parting. In conclusion, let me say that if the present membership, with its experience and added facilities for carrying on the work of the Lord in the years to come, be as faithful as the older members were during the same number of years now past, the city of Syracuse will not long be left with a single organization, but with a number of them. When the reunion of all who have participated in this grand work shall take place, may I be among the happy throng."

W. A. BELDING.

TROY, N. Y., May 28, 1891.

COPY OF TESTIMONIALS PRESENTED TO THE DOCTOR
BY THE CHURCH AT SYRACUSE, N. Y., AT THE
CLOSE OF HIS LABORS THERE.

To Bro. W. A. Belding: —In behalf of the
church of Syracuse, I wish to say that we desire
on this occasion to acknowledge our [indebtedness
to you for the great work that has been achieved
here, by the blessing of God, through your instrumentality.

Words fail to express the emotion of our hearts
and the gratitude we feel for the untiring devotion
with which you have labored among us.   We owe
our existence as a church to your labors.   Many
of us, had it not been for the word of life which
you have preached so faithfully, would have been
at this time without hope and without God in the
world.   Thanks to his holy name, in his providence he saw fit to send you here to preach the
unsearchable riches of Christ.   We would further
say that, like the apostle to the Gentiles, you
"have not shunned to declare all the counsel
of God."   .

While we acknowledge our indebtedness to you,
we feel that it is not in our power to recompense
you ; but you *shall* be recompensed at the resurrection of the just.   Although we have the promise
of a hundred-fold in this life, yet we are told that
we have but a foretaste—"an earnest of the in-
heritance prepared for the saints in light."

The relations you have sustained to us, and the

faithfulness with which you have discharged the obligations which that relationship imposed, have made an impression on our hearts which time will hardly eradicate..

We have no desire to forget you, neither would we be forgotten by you. Therefore we have thought best to present you these vessels [a silver pitcher and goblets] as a token of remembrance and a slight appreciation of what you have done for us.   J. C. HUTCHINGS, Committee.

AUGUST 30, 1864.

CHAPTER XXIII.

THE next work which occupied the doctor's attention for any great length of time was the building of a church at Troy, N. Y. But several important events must be sketched before we follow him to Troy.

In 1862, his son, Rufus E., was married to Martha A. Seymour, of Meridian, Cayuga Co., N. Y. Two days later (January 8) the doctor was himself again married; this time to Miss Emily Sherman, who lived at Pittstown, about twelve miles northeast of Troy. She was one of a family of eight, having four sisters and two brothers. The sisters—Sarah, Asenath, Amanda and Mary—have all been helpful to the work in Eastern New York, contributing most liberally to all necessary funds.

Mrs. Belding, owing to the doctor's migrating life, has mostly always made her home at Pittstown. Together they managed the large and fine farm known as the "Sherman girls'" farm— known far and wide as the seat of the most generous hospitality and of an overflowing abundance, which it was the delight of the sisters to share with their numerous guests. It was the Mecca of the writer's boyhood days. I looked forward to spending a portion of each vacation there with keen anticipation of the welcome always given, and of the lavish table that appealed so strongly to my appetite. Mrs. Belding's last sister, Mary, died March 12, 1897. The farm spoken of is now managed by Mrs. Belding and her son, Sherman W.

Such was the family into which the doctor married, and a most happy marriage it proved, though differing from the home life enjoyed by others. During the time that intervened between his work at Syracuse and that at Troy, he made a flying trip to Chicago to hold a meeting. There was quite a little organization at Chicago, which met in the Opera-house on Clark Street.

The doctor preached on Sunday morning and evening in the Opera-house, and on the week days at the homes of some of the brethren.

One evening he asked the members present why they did not own a house in which to worship. The reply was: "We are not able." The doctor answered: "If I were to say that of you, you would resent it. If you will take hold, I'll see what we can do towards raising a fund for building." Several agreed to do what they could, though doubtful of the result.

The next morning he went into the office of Dr. Major, then a wealthy physician, whose office was in the Opera-house. Seating himself at a desk, Dr. Belding drew up a subscription for a church edifice, and, handing it to Dr. Major, said: " Is that all right?" After reading it, he replied: "Yes." "Then sign it." A moment's deliberation, and Dr. Major's signature for one thousand dollars headed the list. As the doctor did not pick up the book, or look as though he were pleased, Bro. Major inquired: " What is the matter? What did you expect?"

The doctor responded: " If we are men, let's be men—not boys. You ought to give five thousand dollars at least, and as much more as you can afford." After a few moments' conversation, the sum subscribed was changed to five thousand.

Next the doctor took the book to the office of Bro. Hónore (the father of Mrs. Potter Palmer). He looked at the subscription of Dr. Major, and simply ejaculating "My gracious!" put down his own name for a similar amount.

Within ten days the list footed seventeen thousand dollars, and the house of the Lutherans on Randolph Street was purchased. For this fourteen thousand dollars was paid, while one thousand was expended in remodeling it.

The congregation then offered the doctor a salary of twenty-five hundred dollars to preach for them one year. But he replied: " I have promised the Lord that, if spared, I would do a certain work in Troy; I must be about it."

He went to Troy soon after, and labored to organize the church at that place. He succeeded in building them an edifice costing twenty-one thousand dollars, for which labor he received his compensation of five hundred dollars per annum from the Missionary Society of New York State.

Troy is the county-seat of Rensselaer County, N. Y., on the east bank of the Hudson River, and, on account of its location between the hills, which rise somewhat abruptly on that side of the river, its greatest length is from north to south, parallel to the river. It was a manufacturing city of considerable importance, promising at one time to become the center of the iron industries of this country. But the invention of a process that utilized the magnetic ores changed this prospect and ruined the iron manufactories already built. The business of stove manufacturing in Troy was at one time the largest in the world, but strikes and labor unions caused those interested to move to other places, and Cleveland, Detroit and various small Western towns profited by Troy's loss. Shirt and collar making has increased, however, and Troy leads all places in these lines. There is no other place in New York State where girls and women have the opportunities for self-support afforded by this city.

The surrounding country is hilly, and contains some of the best farming land of the State.

We have already spoken of Pittstown, the home of Mrs. Belding. Three miles from this home is the village of Pittstown Corners, a mere "cross-roads," with blacksmith's shop, one or two stores, and possibly one hundred inhabitants. But that little village had a Disciple church long before Troy did, and at one time had the strongest organization in the State.

In the year 1865, Bro. William B. Mooklar, of Covington, Ky., sent to the doctor two young men and the sum of seven hundred dollars, with the message: "Use this and these for the good of the cause." The doctor had become interested in the work of the little band at Troy, N. Y., and, dividing this money, he sent one of the young preachers to Buffalo, N. Y., and the other, Bro. J. Z. Taylor, to Troy.

As the doctor was connected with the Troy Church for the ensuing ten years, we will sketch briefly its record up to the time that his own efforts commence.

As far back as 1844, an organization existed in Troy under charge of four elders, who alternated in preaching the Word. The names of but two of these leaders are now known—Elder Ager and Elder Read. The congregation met in the upper story of a frame building at the corner of River and King Streets, where is now located one of Troy's most prominent banks.

The little band lost in number, and was twice reorganized—the second time having but three or four of the original members among those comprising the new organization. Soon after this reorganization, Dr. Belding became interested in the work, and sent Bro. J. Z. Taylor to hold a meeting for them. This meeting was held in the Young Men's Association Hall on First Street, over the old post-office. This hall would seat twelve hundred people, and was consequently much too large for the little band and the few friends they could gather together. In spite of this, a good meeting was held. But, for some reason, Bro. Taylor could not stay, and Dr. Belding sent D. R. Van Buskirk to continue the work.

Bro. Van Buskirk commenced in August or

September, 1865, and remained two months. During his stay, Dr. Belding made one of his unexpected trips, and, arriving in Troy in the afternoon a short time before the time for meeting, he went to the building. Before he had time to make himself known, he was accosted by a little daughter of Captain Rhodes, who said: "We are having some *very* interesting meetings upstairs ; wouldn't you like to go up?" "I don't know but I will," responded the doctor. He gravely went up with her, to be warmly welcomed as an old and needed friend. The doctor spoke of this incident, and promised the brethren that if they would have the cause as closely at heart as that young girl, they would soon have a church building to meet in.

At this time—besides the church at Pittstown Corners, already spoken of—there were congregations at Eagle Mills and Poestenkill, both small towns, four to eight miles east of Troy.

CHAPTER XXIV.

THE Troy membership numbered eighteen, and at the close of D. R. Van Buskirk's efforts, in November, the doctor began to look for some smaller place in which to worship. Finally, about May, 1866, he secured Agricultural Hall, at the corner of Ferry and First Streets, where they worshiped for some time.

June 2, a legal notice having been given, the members of the church of Christ met at their place of worship. The pastor, Dr. W. A. Belding, presiding, Cornelius Van Schaick and John C. Welch were selected as judges of election, and three trustees were elected: Joseph H. Rhodes, for the term of three years; Jeremiah Washburn for two years, and James B. Thomas for one year.

A document was drawn up in proper form, for record in the county of Rensselaer, containing the names of trustees and adopting the name, Church of Christ of Troy, N. Y., "which name it is to be forever called." Thus was the foundation laid, legally and in good order. A nucleus of eighteen members was formed to accomplish what the citizens of Troy universally said could not be done; *i. e.*, the building of another church.

The newspapers resented the sending of a missionary to Troy. They for some time kept up a fusillade of sarcasm that was more annoying than harmful. The doctor finally wrote and had published an article in which he stated that Troy certainly needed missionaries, for some of the inhabitants acted like heathens.

The doctor promptly opened a subscription-book for purchasing a lot on which to build a house of worship. The sum of five thousand, three hundred and twenty-one dollars was subscribed within a short time, and the selection of a lot located suitably for church purposes occupied his attention. Troy had been through a terrible fire only a short time before (1862), and there were then many vacant lots formerly occupied by buildings. The southwest corner of Seventh and Fulton Streets was selected and purchased.

The old subscription-book lies before us as we write, and is headed with the names of W. A. Belding, Mrs. W. A. Belding and Asenath and Sarah Sherman.

In the records of the many different enterprises in which the doctor was engaged we find him not content to devote time and energy to the work, but he was liberal with his money. Almost invariably his name would head the list and the names of his family or of his wife's sisters would appear next.

Subscriptions were now taken for the erection of a building, and were due and payable when the walls were up ready for the roof.

The first subscription for the purchase of a lot was made June 9, 1866, and the date of the first meeting in the church was 1868. This took place in the basement, the upper story not being completed. But soon after the edifice was declared

complete, and it was announced that a total of
twenty-one thousand dollars had been spent and
that a debt of three thousand dollars remained.
This may seem a high price for the Troy property, but this was soon after the war, and materials
and labor were very expensive.

In 1883 this building was sold to the Lutherans
for twelve thousand five hundred dollars, and the
congregation built the one now occupied at the
corner of River and Jay Streets.

It must not be supposed that during these years
the doctor had been constantly in Troy. Scarcely
a week went by without a drive to Pittstown. He
owned a horse and carriage which he kept for
that trip alone. Meetings were held at Amster-
dam and elsewhere, and his financial work for
the missionary societies was kept up.

In 1870, at his solicitation, his son Rufus, with
his wife and family (composed of two sons, Warren S. and Paul W.), moved from Syracuse to
Troy. The doctor, soon after, purchased a home,
in which they still reside (1897). The doctor
had now two homes, and alternated between them
according to the promptings of his restless nature.

CHAPTER XXV.

THE church of Christ in Brooklyn is the outgrowth of a movement made by a number of honest, conscientious, Bible-loving Baptists, to escape from the bonds of sectarianism, under the lead of their pastor, Mr. J. Bradford Cleaver, whom the Sixth Avenue Baptist Church had tried and found guilty of the heinous crime of having declared that he would baptize a young lady upon a confession of her faith in Christ, without submitting her rights in the premises to any church.

A considerable number left that organization with him and they established a "Gospel Church," upon a declaration of their belief in the sufficiency of the Bible alone as a rule of faith.

Mr. Cleaver had not received a theological education, consequently he had little to unlearn. But, having been trained for the bar, and being successful in the practice of law, he had acquired the habits of analysis. Looking upon the Bible as a book of statutes, instead of a repository of texts to sustain preconceived theories, before he was aware of the fact he found himself in the ranks of the Disciples of Christ, manfully battling for the faith delivered to the saints. When apprised of his position and the logical result, he did not draw back, but continued to search the Scriptures. Having learned to "rightly divide the word," he became more and more impressed with the beauty and simplicity of the plan of human redemption, as revealed in the King's

(103)

statute-book, and brought to light by those whom the world calls "Campbellites."

Some of those who followed him into the "Gospel Church," not having moral courage suffi- cient to sustain them under such insolent epi- thets, drew back and returned to sectarianism.

In August, 1875, while spending his vacation in Troy, Mr. Cleaver was invited to speak for the church there. This he did with such satisfac- tion to the members assembled that he was in- duced to remain there until February, 1877. Dur- ing his ministry in Troy some one hundred and twenty-nine were added to their number.

After Mr. Cleaver left Brooklyn, meetings were continued in the chapel on Lincoln Place until about the middle of November, 1875, at which time, by a vote of its members, the "Gospel Church" was disbanded and in its stead they organized a church of Christ.

They chose Dr. Belding as pastor and he labored there until October 1, 1876. His efforts to raise money to build or buy a church were, as usual, successful. In this work he was warmly seconded by Brethren G. B. Farrington, C. C. Martin and others. The result was that they bought a house of the Methodists. This was on Sterling Place, well located and beautifully constructed, having originally cost fifty-seven thousand dollars. For this house they paid twelve thousand dollars and assumed a mortgage of six thousand.

In 1876 the doctor resigned his pastorate for the reason that he had resolved, early in his min-

isterial life, that he would never have it said of
him: "He is too old to preach."

The age he fixed upon as that in which to close
his settled pastoral work was sixty years. That
time had now arrived, and since that day he has
had no time engagements with any church. He
has remained for months preaching for one
church, but the engagement has been considered
as from week to week. The church prospered
steadily, though under the care of several pastors who remained but a short time each. At
the conclusion of the engagement of Bro. J.
Z. Tyler, who had been located with them for
two years, a call was given to Bro. C. B. Edgar,
of Kentucky. He was delayed by sickness, and
the doctor was asked to preach during this inter-
val. He responded, and for six months preached
regularly, receiving for compensation forty dollars a week.

Nothing was ever said by him or to him regarding salary while in Brooklyn; but during his first
stay the clerk had handed him fifteen dollars
every Sunday evening, this being doubtless all
they could then afford.

The change from a little band of about thirty,
with no home, to a fine building and increased
membership, was very encouraging. From that
time the organization has continually prospered.

Greenpoint Mission occupied the time and en-
ergies of the doctor for one year. It was an out-
lying point of Brooklyn, between four and five
miles from the Sterling Place church. The neigh-

borhood was full of churches and was sparsely settled, while the people were poor. The mission was started by the Sterling Place congregation and assisted somewhat by the New York Missionary Society. They numbered about twenty and met in a store-room, having no organization whatever. But, when left by the doctor, they numbered nearly one hundred, met in a house of their own that had cost fifteen hundred dollars, and were thoroughly organized.

This work was very trying to the doctor. While at Greenpoint he lost flesh and was half sick most of the time. He describes it as a great deal of work with very little results. Many pledges were found uncollectable, and there was little effort made to pay him anything for his time and labor; but with dogged perseverance he put them on their feet and left them prosperous and out of debt.

CHAPTER XXVI

In the winter of 1877, Dr. Belding received a joint letter written by Ovid Butler and O. A. Burgess and asking him to come over to Indianapolis. He went and found present the subscribers to a fund (then small) to establish an institute in the South for the education of the colored race.

Officers were elected and the doctor was requested to assume the responsibility of raising the necessary funds. He replied: "I am under obligations to the Missionary Society, but will divide my time between their work and yours, if you wish." It was so agreed, and he commenced a work that has always had for him a great attraction. It resulted in the establishing of a school which has given instruction to over *six thousand* colored pupils of both sexes, who would probably have gone through life in complete mental and moral ignorance, had it not been for this work.

A school was started in two dilapidated school buildings in Jackson, Miss. These structures were owned by the Quakers, who gave free use of them. Bro. R. Faurot and wife taught there while a permanent place was being decided upon.

April 27, 1882, the doctor called on Mr. T. I. Martin, of Louisville, Ky. This gentleman owned a plantation of eight hundred acres at Edwards, Hinds Co., Miss. This plantation he held for sale at fifteen thousand dollars. But, after talking with the doctor and learning the use for which he desired it, he said that he would donate one-half of the amount, making the cost to the society seven thousand dollars. A bargain was concluded on that basis, the doctor entering into a contract making him personally responsible for the payment of that sum. July 5, the deed was given and (including what had been paid at the drawing up of the contract) the sum of four thousand dollars was paid, and a trust deed to secure the remaining three thousand dollars, due in one, two and three years, was given.

The doctor says of Mr. Martin: "He was my ideal of a business man—liberal, unsuspicious, but business-like."

This plantation is declared to be equal to an endowment fund of thirty thousand dollars. It has been, to a great extent, the support of the institution, pupils paying for their tuition by an hour's labor, daily, during the school term.

The school was moved from Jackson to the plantation, which was named Mount Beulah. Bro. Faurot died in October, about three months after the purchase of the plantation. The interests of the school staggered under the blow. The doctor was telegraphed for. He came, and, in the work that he found it necessary to do, he became ill. For several weeks he was confined to his bed with a slow fever. This was a natural result of the change of climate, as he is peculiarly susceptible to hot weather, always suffering in health during the heated spells of summer. He was most kindly cared for and has often expressed his appreciation of the attention he received. Upon his recovery he set earnestly to work to supply the place left vacant by the death of Bro. Faurot.

An arrangement was finally entered into with Bro. Jeptha Hobbs, of Kentucky, to take the presidency of the Institute. This he did about the last of the year (1882), the contract being for five years. The terms were that he was to run the school and pay all expenses himself, for which he received the use of the farm. All cash contributed to the work (now known as the Southern Christian Institute) was to be devoted to permanent improvements; all other donations were to be for his own use. He faithfully carried out his contract, and the school and plantation both prospered under his management.

In the appendix will be found a description of the plantation written by a correspondent of the New York *Herald* and published in that paper in 1883; also, an abstract of the origin, aims and purposes of the Institute, as given in their prospectus of 1887.

Towards the last of 1887, Dr. Belding closed his connection with the Institute. Several thousand dollars were due him, for which he took various notes, most of which were payable after the death of the makers. These notes had been obtained by him for the Institute and were, of course, rather uncertain assets. He also turned over to the General Missionary Society (which assumed the work) between seventy-five and eighty shares of the stock, which cost him fifty dollars per share.

It has been the same in every work in which he has been engaged—he took what compensation was offered, and then helped liberally, with no thought of his own needs.

CHAPTER XXVII.

In July, 1883, a call to "come and aid us in San Francisco" was heard and heeded by the doctor. Leaving, temporarily, the work of the Southern Christian Institute, in which he was then engaged, he started for California, where he labored until March 29, 1884. This trip is one of which the memories are very pleasant, and good were the results of his work while there. A lot was purchased and paid for, and a balance of nearly three thousand dollars remained in the treasury. (Total, about nine thousand five hundred dollars.)

On the last evening of his stay, a farewell reception was tendered him, and he was the recipient of a fine gold-mounted cane, having engraved on its head, "To Dr. W. A. Belding, by San Francisco friends."

In a letter written from Dallas, Tex., soon after, the doctor says: "I have been caned at home and in private, but never publicly before. But 'twas kindly done, and tears were in my eyes and also in the eyes of most of those assembled. Oh, these meetings and partings of friends—especially the partings." F. W. Pattee took charge of the San Francisco congregation, and the farewell to the doctor served as a welcome to him and his wife.

The trip east was by way of Los Angeles and the Southern Pacific Railroad, with a stop over Lord's Day at Dallas, Tex., and a few days at

Mt. Beulah, where he found the school flourishing. The month of May finds him at Pittstown with wife and son.

Englewood, then a suburb of Chicago, was the scene of his labors in 1887. In July of that year, he undertook to build a house for a little band who met on Sixty-third Street in a rented store. During a stay of six months, he bought a lot, built, furnished and paid for a house, and interested the Chicago churches in, and formed, a city board of missions. This board is composed of two members chosen from each church organization within the city of Chicago, and additional members from congregations numbering over one hundred. The duty and object of the board was to select mission points, appoint persons to take charge of these missions, and look after their financial support—in short, to increase the number of churches in Chicago. This board has not only helped establish the Englewood church, but has a North and a West Side mission, both progressing nicely.

In the appendix will be found a copy of a testimonial presented the doctor by this board, showing their appreciation of his efforts in the difficult work of raising money in Englewood.

It will be remembered by the reader that he raised the money to purchase the first church of the Disciples in Chicago. Adding that to these later labors will explain why, of all cities, his welcome is perhaps warmest in the "city by the lake."

W. H. Rogers, in his Boston letter to the *Missionary Weekly* (October, 1888), reporting the annual meeting at Worcester, speaks of the doctor in a way that evidences the feeling regarding him possessed by all who have known him and his work. It follows:

"The Disciples of New England had their annual festival at Worcester from Friday, September 28, until Monday, October 1, closing with their highly prized farewell meeting, Monday morning.

"Bro. W. A. Belding preached on Friday night and hastened to Brooklyn the next morning. Bro. Belding is venerable according to the almanac only. In face, in spirit, in faith, in hope, and in cheerfulness, in energy as well as in general movements of the body, he is still in his prime. He is a sort of patron saint in the hearts of the Worcester brethren. In his Christian make-up he unites the rocky firmness of the olden time with the catholicity and growth of the modern period. The older brethren trust him, while the younger brethren rejoice in him as their own. Few men among us have raised more money for religious, educational and benevolent purposes than he, and with his own hands he has buried some ten thousand believing penitents with their Lord in baptism.

"The time was when he knew personally almost every one of our preachers, and it is an evidence of our growth that now there are so many among us who have never seen his face."

The doctor now lives at Pittstown with his wife and son, Sherman W., who also has a wife and two young sons.

He preaches on Lord's Day for the little congregation at Pittstown Corners, and occasionally breaks the monotony by attending or holding a meeting elsewhere. A man of eighty, he still holds his faculties unimpaired, and his form is almost as straight as of yore. His endurance is somewhat lessened of late, but his hair remains dark, and his eyesight is better than it has been for years. He has discarded glasses altogether, and, were it not for a slight deafness, his friends could not see that time had touched him.

Verily a sweet and pleasant journey on the downhill side of life is his, surrounded by his family, with no recent gaps in their little circle ; with the family of his eldest son, Rufus, near him, at Troy, and hosts of friends and brethren glad to see him wherever he goes ; and with the proud consciousness that he has been of use in the world in the cause he espoused.

APPENDIX.

GENEALOGY OF BELDING FAMILY.

RICHARD AND WILLIAM BAYLDON (BROTHERS) WERE AMONG THE EARLIEST SETTLERS OF WETHERSFIELD, CONN.,

1640.

WILLIAM BAYLDON
moved to Norwalk with family
1646.

Samuel, John, Mary, DANIEL, Susaunna, Nathaniel.
b. 1648

Nathaniel, Daniel, John, SAMUEL, Richard, John, William, and seven daughters.
b. 1687

SAMUEL.
b. 1729

DANIEL, John.
b. 1754

Alfred, Amos, Allen, RUFUS, Sears.
b. 1778   d. 1854

Ruth, Charlotte, Martha, Anson, Edwin C., WARREN ASA, Alvin, Sabin, Louisa.
b. 1816

Rufus E. and five who died young (by first wife).   Sherman W. (by second wife).
b. 1841   b. 1868

Warren S.,   Paul W.,   Louis K.,   Anson W.   Victor L.,   Leroy S.
b. 1862   b. 1868   b. 1876   b. 1881   b. 1895   b. March 5, 1897

Myra E.
b. 1884

A TROY CHAPLAIN PRAYS FOR THE LOBBY.

[From the Troy " Times."]

Rev. Dr. Belding, of this city, offered prayer in the Assembly on Friday last. The correspondent of the New York *Times* says of him :

"Among the chaplains who are in the habit of alternately offering prayer in this Legislature, Rev. Dr. Belding, of Troy, appears most clearly to comprehend the situation, and to direct his petitions to a quarter where they are most needed. He seldom comes down here to officiate as chaplain, but, when he does, he hits the nail on the head every time. In opening the Assembly this morning he prayed, among other things, that ' the men who are in the habit of loitering about the halls of the Legislature with bribery in their hands might be induced to see the error of their ways, and that their wicked designs, if they had any, might be thwarted.' There was no response to this appeal either from members or lobbyists, but the people from the State at large will no doubt second the petition of Rev. Dr. Belding."

(117)

PIONEER PREACHERS.

The recent death of J. J. Moss has called my attention again to the rapidly vanishing number of Disciple preachers who were well known and active on the Western Reserve. Among these J. J. Moss was one of the earliest and one of the strongest. My father heard him preach for the first time in Randolph, Portage County, in August of the year 1832. At this meeting W. A. Belding, whose name should appear in the list of the preachers fairly called pioneers, was baptized.

Bro. Belding baptized me. I made the first exhortation I ever tried to make, at a meeting in North Royalton, where he was preaching, and his name for me is written large in the honored list of the pioneers. Bro. Belding has baptized more than ten thousand persons, and has been in the ministry almost sixty years. J. M. Monroe, in his brief notice of his uncle, J. J. Moss, speaks of J. H. Jones as the only survivor of the pioneer preachers of the Western Reserve. But there still lives W. A. Belding, who is nearly eighty years of age; Wm. Moody, hale and hearty at eighty-five; P. Green, who will soon enter his eighty-fifth year, and J. H. Jones. In regard to Bro. Moss, it was my privilege on his eightieth birthday to make, in behalf of many friends, an address congratulating him on his having reached the age of fourscore. He was a sturdy disciple of the Lord. His ambition to extend the kingdom of Christ was as restless as that of Alexander of

Macedon, and his courage in facing every enemy of the truth was equal to that of Julius Cæsar.

It will not be long before the last of those glorious men will be known only in the memories that remain and never die. May we, their sons and grandsons, be as faithful to our generations as they were to theirs.   F. M. GREEN.

WILMINGTON, O., June 22, 1895.

TESTIMONIAL TO DR. W. A. BELDING.

CITY BOARD OF CHRISTIAN MISSIONS,
CHICAGO, JANUARY 9, 1888

WHEREAS, Our beloved brother, Dr. W. A. Belding, did, at the earnest and combined solicitation of this Board and the congregation of disciples in Englewood, undertake the laborious work of securing for said congregation a house of worship; and,

WHEREAS, This undertaking has involved on the part of our brother a protracted absence of months from his distant home and family; and,

WHEREAS, His endeavors have been crowned with abundant and marked success, wherein we do greatly rejoice and pay humble tribute to the God of all grace; therefore be it

Resolved, That not only do we desire to place on record our entire approval and satisfaction with his work, but that our heartfelt thanks and grateful appreciation be hereby tendered him for the unselfish devotion he has exhibited in this enterprise, and for the sacrifice he has made in order to its accomplishment.

Be it further resolved, That a copy of these resolutions be furnished Bro. Belding.

H. H. HUBBARD, ⎱ Com.
W. P. KEELER, ⎰

(120)

SOUTHERN CHRISTIAN INSTITUTE.

[From the New York "Herald."]

The name of Hinds County, Miss., is historic in connection with the riots of 1876, wherein the colored voters were driven to the swamps. It is one of the centers of black population. Twenty years ago General Grant had crossed the Mississippi below Vicksburg, moved on eastward, and many a soldier still remembers the battle of Champion Hills. Nearly three thousand men were buried on the field. The enemy fell back toward Big Black River. At McGee farm the struggle was sharp, and there shot and shell have been thrown from the ditches dug to drain the cotton fields, now cultivated by the free labor of black men, who, after that, were made Union soldiers.

A great plantation house stood on a beautiful eminence overlooking the Vicksburg road and the Black River. In the front was a wide lawn and on the east a garden of flowers, while in the rear southward was a cotton-gin and rows of negro cabins. It was known as the Cook plantation of two thousand acres or more. The owner mustered his slaves, and the cotton grew in fields miles away toward sunset along the Black River. The woman of the mansion commanded its halls, and there are tales of tying the negroes to the shade trees, and in the strength of her own arm lashing them with the whip. How swift came the retribution! Call it providence, call it fate,

call it what you may.   Cannon balls fell close on
that house.   A water pond near by was drained,
and in its mire a solid shot had lain these twenty
years.   The soldiers bivouacked in the woods
southwest.   Names and dates cut in the trees in
1861–63 still show plainly.

The mansion was used for a hospital.   The
spring by the river bank gave water to friend and
foe.   The plantation was stripped and its owner
gone   The railroad bridge at the river was de-
stroyed, but Grant marched on.   We all know
the result of that march, and the siege which
followed.

The Southern Christian Institute has it in control now.   Two hundred boys and girls have been
taught to study within its walls the past winter.

If one is up at sunrise here, he finds the morning light breaking over the little town of Edwards,
on the east.   It is a great cotton market.   Near
the mansion now occupied for the colored school
is some trace of the grand garden of former days.
A close line of cedar-trees partly hides it on the
east, and central through the ground from north
to south are ridges thrown up for beds of flowers.
On the north side all there is left to mark the
fearful days of the olden times is a single rose-
tree, or rather a dense clump of the Cherokee
rose, which stands six to ten feet high, and covers
a spot, say fifty feet square.   It was covered
with buds just ready for bloom, and in a few
days would be one solid ball of white roses.   We
measured a square of the buds in sight, and

counted in order to estimate the bloom. It will blossom a half-million roses. From the delightful site of the mansion the plantation stretches westward away to the clumps of shade trees by the river. It reminds us of the Garfield farm at Mentor, and the railway cuts through from east to west going to Vicksburg.

The Southern Christian Institute originated with Thomas Munnell and others in 1873. He was then secretary of the General Christian Missionary Convention. Through the labors of George Owen (white) and Levin Wood (colored) many freedmen in Mississippi became disciples. Twenty or thirty churches were formed, or came in a body from the Baptists. To render this work permanent and effective, Munnell foresaw there must be a class of preachers and Sunday-school teachers much better educated than any those days furnished. To supply this need, he projected the Southern Christian Institute. In connection with his general work, he made two trips to Mississippi about this time to push forward the work.

By special act of the Legislature, he obtained a charter, drafted by Ovid Butler, of Indianapolis, approved March 5, 1875, authorizing an organization on a stock basis of not less than ten thousand dollars in fifty-dollar shares, and exempting all property, both personal and real, to the amount of two hundred and fifty thousand dollars, from all taxes whatever.

Through the personal solicitations of George

Owen, Thomas Munnell and Dr. W. A. Belding, the minimum quantity of stock was taken. At Indianapolis, December 4, 1877, the company organized and elected trustees. Dr. Belding was made financial agent.

SALVATION.

"Wherefore he is able also to save to the uttermost them who come unto God by him, seeing he ever liveth to make intercession for them" (Heb. vii. 25).

The idea of salvation suggests danger. If there were no danger, there would be no need of salvation. Let us first inquire what the salvation referred to in the text involves.

A salvation to the uttermost can mean nothing less than a salvation from everything which annoys or makes unhappy, and these can be summed up in four things—sin, disease, death and the grave. Or, in other words, from the love of sin, the practice of sin, the guilt of sin and the consequences of sin.

Of whom does the writer speak? Of Jesus of Nazareth, of whom the angel told his mother: "Thou shalt call his name Jesus, for he shall save his people from their sins."

The next question is, Is he able to do it? Go with me to the bedside of the paralytic, and hear Jesus saying to him, "Thy sins are all forgiven thee," and when he discovers among those gathered about, them who doubted as to his power to forgive sins, he says, "Whether is it easier for me to say, Thy sins are all forgiven; or to say, Arise, take up thy bed, and walk?" and that they might know that he had power on earth to forgive sins, he says to the sick man: "Arise, take up thy bed, and walk." Thus he demonstrates his power over sin and disease.

(125)

But, again, he meets the funeral procession, which he commands to stop. They are bearing to the lonely grave the only son of a widowed mother. He calls him back to life and presents him to his mother living and well.

Still again, we follow him to the grave of Lazarus. He stops and sheds tears of sympathy with the weeping sisters, for the record says: "Jesus wept." Then, lifting up his heart and voice in solemn prayer to his Father in heaven, he says, "Father, hear me;" then, turning to the grave in which the dead man lay, speaks with a voice that not only penetrates the dark recesses of the tomb, but also the dull ear of the dead man, "Lazarus, come forth," and said to those weeping ones, "Unbind him, and let him go." He has now demonstrated his power over all the enemies of humanity which can afflict or make them unhappy in this world or any other.

Next we inquire, Is he willing? Yes, for he invites all who are weary and heavy laden to come unto him. John, in the Book of Revelation, says: "The Spirit and the bride say, Come. Let him that heareth say, Come. Let him that is athirst come. And whosoever will, let him take the water of life freely." We have learned that he is both able and willing; thank God. If now we can find out the conditions of this, the most precious gift of God to man, and find in our own hearts a willingness to accept the gift upon God's own terms, we are nigh the kingdom of God.

We learn from Paul, in the same letter from

which we have selected our text, that Jesus, "although a son, learned obedience by the things which he suffered, and became the author of eternal salvation to those who obey him." Also, in closing up God's Book, we are told in language which can not be misunderstood that those who do his commandments are blessed, and shall be permitted to partake of the tree of life, and to enter through the gates into the city, the disobedient and wicked shut out. (Rev. xxii. 14, 15.) I now speak with reverence, and say that God can not save to the uttermost, or save from sin, without saving from its love, its practice, its guilt and its consequences, from the first three in this world and life, and from the fourth and last in the world and life to come.

As the God of nature is the God of religion, and all blessings in the realm of nature are conditional, why is it unreasonable to suppose that all spiritual blessings are also conditional? The question is, How does he propose to save men from the love of sin? I answer unhesitatingly, by faith. Faith in what or whom? Not in a dogma, not in a church, but in a person—"Jesus the Christ as the Son of God, divine as well as human ; faith in him as the only Savior." " God so loved the world that he gave his only begotten Son, that whosoever believeth in him might not perish, but have everlasting life."

This faith begets such love in the heart that it destroys, or saves from, the love of sin. No more can the love of God and the love of sin dwell in the same heart at the same time than light and darkness in the same room. None can be saved from sin without being saved from its practice. What is the condition? I speak the sentiment of the Bible when I say, repentance. "Except ye repent, ye shall all likewise perish," says Jesus.

I have often asked, " What is repentance?" and nearly as often get the answer, "It is sorrow." But another says it is "godly sorrow," and that is not all, for Paul declares that "godly sorrow worketh repentance that needs not to be repented of."

The Scriptural meaning of. repentance, then, is a sorrow for sin, a determination to forsake it, and that determination put in practice as the good Book teaches. "Let the wicked man forsake his way, and the unrighteous his thoughts; return unto the Lord, who will have mercy, and unto our God, who will abundantly pardon." Who will deny that this repentance will save from the practice of sin?

The next question, and a very important one, is, when a person is saved from the love of sin by faith and the practice by repentance, is he necessarily saved from its guilt? The answer is no. Permit me to illustrate. I do not offer this as proof, but simply to get the thought before the reader. Suppose you were dealing in goods, and my habit has been to purchase on credit; I at once decide to buy no more on credit, and in the future pay for every article which I purchase.

This resolution is fully carried out ; does this cancel or pay the debts of the past? If so, it might be an easy way of paying debts, but I think not very satisfactory to the one who holds the claim. Now, its application is readily discovered. Here is a man who has spent many years of his life in sin. In hearing or reading of the love of God manifested to man in the gift of his only Son to save a perishing world, his understanding is enlightened, his affections captivated, he finds and acknowledges himself a sinner, and forms the resolution, I will try to be a better man. Now, suppose he could live and does without committing another sin during his whole life, what is to become of those he has committed? One of three things may be done : make an atonement (pay the debt), which, if he can do, no need of a Savior ; they may be forgiven, or stand upon the books against him forever.

Thanks to our kind Father, who proposes to forgive, and he has told us in his word (Heb. ix. 22) that "without the shedding of blood there is no remission." He also assures us in the same connection that the blood of animals could not purge from sin ; nothing short of the blood of Christ could cleanse from its guilt. This is the sentiment of all who accept the sacrificial offering of Christ, but when and where and how this is applied is the question to which I would invite the reader's most careful and candid consideration. Let me ask the thoughtful, When was that blood shed? Was it not in his death, and more than eighteen hundred years ago? Who, then, can expect a literal application of his blood? It is by faith the blood is sprinkled on the heart, but when and where? When we approach his death, and in the language of Paul (Rom. vi. 1–4) by being baptized into it, or, as Paul affirms (Heb. x. 22) : " Having our hearts sprinkled from an evil conscience, and our bodies washed with pure water." Now the question may arise in the mind, With what is the heart sprinkled? Peter answers that question in his first letter: " Elect according to the foreknowledge of God the Father, through sanctification of the Spirit, unto obedience and sprinkling of the blood of Jesus Christ" (1 Peter i. 2).

As we have learned that the sinner is saved from the love of sin by faith, from the practice of sin by repentance, and from the guilt of sin by the blood of Christ, all this is in this life, and we now feel anxious to know how we can continue in this saved state, and enjoy the full fruition " or salvation to the uttermost " which God has promised, for we are still exposed to and afflicted by the consequences of sin, which are disease, death and the grave. The good man dies ; the innocent and unconscious babe dies. If the Christian is overtaken in a fault, John tells us in his first letter (1 John i. 9), writing to Christians: " If we confess our sins, he is faithful and just to forgive us our sins, and to cleanse us from all unrighteousness."

Thus we discover that prayers preceded by

faith, repentance and confession are the conditions upon which the believing, penitent and baptized person is promised forgiveness. When Simon the sorcerer had believed and was baptized, he committed sin in supposing that the miraculous gift could be purchased with money, and Peter (Acts viii. 22) commands him to " repent, and pray God that the thoughts of his heart might be forgiven." Not for the forgiveness of all the sins of his life, for he had secured this by accepting Christ and complying (as he was taught) with the conditions which Jesus himself had commanded the apostles to proclaim (Mark xvi. 16), " He that believeth and is baptized shall be saved," and the record says Simon did believe and was baptized, and if the Savior's words were true, he was saved from past sins, and yet like all others in this life exposed to the consequences of sin, from which he must be saved in order to enjoy the full salvation, or that which is to the " uttermost."

This third and last salvation is to be "worked out " as the apostle of Jesus exhorts in Phil. ii. 12 — " work out your own salvation with fear and trembling," etc. We may therefore conclude that the conditions of this final salvation are secured by forming a Christian character. Hence Peter exhorts in his second letter (2 Peter i. 6–11). Add something to your faith. He evidently did not accept the doctrine of " justification by faith only," but believed additions were essential; faith being alone is dead. " Add to your faith virtue [or courage], to virtue knowledge, to knowledge temperance, to temperance patience, to patience brotherly kindness, and to brotherly kindness charity " (or love). These make a perfect character, and secure admission into the everlasting kingdom, for Peter says in the same passage: " If you do these things, you shall never fall, for so an entrance shall be ministered unto you abundantly into the everlasting kingdom of our Lord and Savior Jesus Christ." This salvation is complete, " saved to the uttermost," saved from everything which can annoy or make unhappy, for in that kingdom nothing shall be permitted to enter which can disturb the peace of its inhabitants.

God shall wipe all tears from all faces, and banish sorrow from every heart ; permit his children to look upon his face without an intervening veil, and enjoy his smile forever. There with purified spirits and immortalized bodies, sin forever banished, saved from its love by our faith in Christ, from its practice by repentance, which results in reformation, from its guilt by the blood of Christ (applied by faith when we were baptized into his death), and from its consequences by forming a Christian character.

In conclusion let me ask, Who would not be a Christian? All which is in this world worth possessing belongs to God's children, and all that the heart can desire is promised in the next. Paul, in Rom. viii. 32, asks : " If he that spared not his own Son, but delivered him up for us all, how shall he not with him freely give us all things?'' Again he declares (1 Cor. iii. 21–23) '' that all things are yours; whether Paul, or Apollos, or Cephas, or the world, or life, or death, or things present, or things to come; all are yours; and ye are Christ's; and Christ is God's.'' Christ must reign until all enemies are put under his feet, and when all are subdued, even the last enemy conquered, which is death, then he will deliver up the kingdom to God, even the Father, who shall be all in all. Christ's reign will end, and coming up the golden paved street in the city of our God followed by the blood-washed throng, he introduces them to his Father, saying: '' Here, Father, am I, and the children whom thou hast given me.'' Reader, shall you and I be there? May the Father of all our mercies help us to be ready.

CHRISTIAN UNION.

SERMON BY DR. W. A. BELDING.

["Church Union," May 27, 1876.]

On the natal day of the world's Savior, the angelic choir sang an introductory hymn adapted to his mission: "Glory to God in the highest, peace on earth and good will to men."

In the Savior's memorable prayer, recorded in the seventeenth chapter of John's testimony, he unburdens his almost bursting heart in these impressive words: "I pray not for these alone, but for all them also who shall believe on me through their word, that they all may be one, as thou, Father, art in me, and I in thee, that they also may be one in us, that the world may believe that thou hast sent me."

The oft-repeated sayings of those men whose lips were fired by God's own inspiration in their ministerial labors, give full evidence of their true devotion to the theme: "Mind the same thing"; "Speak the same thing"; "Be of one heart and of one mind"; "Mark them who cause divisions"; "While one says, I am of Paul, and another, I am of Apollos, you walk as men and are carnal." These are but the reiterations of the same sentiment sung by the heavenly choir as it left the plains of Bethlehem for its native home. These utterances were prompted by the same spirit which was breathed forth in the Savior's prayer, and which guided the heavenly messenger

(134)

as he stood beside the loving John upon the Isle of Patmos, and uttered the last words to be revealed to men until the startling cry, "Behold, the bridegroom cometh," and pronounced that terrible denunciation against him who dares "to add to or take away from the words written in this book" (Rev. xxii. 18, 19). The religious world has been made to see, and to deplore deeply, the divided conditions of the so-called church; an interest has been awakened in the hearts of thousands to search for "the old paths," together with a disposition to return to the primitive oneness of the church, established on the first Pentecost after the crucifixion of the world's Redeemer. For this I thank God and take courage.

While so many have discovered the necessity there is for a platform, broad enough and strong enough to hold and carry all the true and loving friends of Jesus, they have failed to see that God has provided such a one, and are themselves making every effort to erect one, which, like themselves, must be too contracted and too weak.

Thus far, the religious world has advanced, and in the right direction. They have organized associations and called conventions—local and general, young men's and old men's, young women's and old women's Christian associations.

When they come from their various religious homes to worship in these associations, they meet to worship the same God, to love and adore the same divine Savior, and enjoy the same blessed and divine Spirit; but when they go out, it is to labor with all their wonted zeal to build higher and stronger these partition walls which have so long kept apart the acknowledged children of the living God. And why all this? Let me tell it in the spirit of my Master, and may you, my dear brother, hear it!

When you go to the place where these associations meet, you leave your "isms" at the door— would that the world could see them as you stack them in the vestibule—Presbyterianism and Methodism, Baptistism and Episcopalianism, Lutheranism and Congregationalism, are all left to rest together quietly in the vestibule, whilst the owners of them are inside, engaged in peaceful worship, wishing the "heavenly meeting would ne'er break up, and the precious Sabbath never end."

Stand at the door until the last sweet hymn is sung, "Blest be the tie that binds our hearts in Christian love"; wait until the last amen is said, "that the peace of God and fellowship of the Divine Spirit may go and abide with the parting ones forever." See the bustle and commotion now. As the passers-by go out, they return to their various churches, perhaps to worship the self-same hour, each eager to gather up the bundle which he brought, and fearful lest he might, perchance, lay his hand upon the package of another, less precious than his own.

Oh, that each one could leave his party name and creed thus laid down, without which he has survived for a few hours, giving them to the devil, where they all belong! Or, what would be better

still, make of them a bonfire, that they may pass
out of sight and forever be forgotten.

Methinks if this were done, shrieks of despair
would be the common wailing of the legions of
the dark abode. There would be more joy among
the heavenly host than even at creation's dawn,
and the angel songsters would strike a still higher
keynote upon their golden harps than when they
sang the birth-song of God's only begotten and
beloved Son. When this shall come to pass—
and for it I will ever pray—"the solitary places
shall be glad, and the deserts blossom as the
rose."

Then hallelujahs shall be shouted from ten thousand tongues which never lisped the praise of
God before. I thank my God there is a common
ground of union, concerning which there is no
controversy. What we need to do, and what
must be done, before the time so anxiously looked
for, and so earnestly prayed for, will come, is to
accept and adopt practically what we all, without
a dissenting voice, admit in theory.

Pile up the many hundred creeds in the so-
called Protestant religious world, lay them on the
precious Bible, and with a ladder, long as Jacob's,
climb to the topmost one, if you can reach it, and
upon its first page you will find the sentence written : " We believe the Bible, the Old and New
Testaments, to be the only infallible rule of faith
and practice. What is not contained therein, and
can not be proven thereby, ought not to be required of any person as an article of faith." Let

us, then, adopt the creed in which we all agree
as the only perfect one, and about which there is
no controversy.

There is also a name which all are willing to
wear, and to which none will object. My Baptist brother might not be willing to accept the one
so gracefully and easily worn by my Presbyterian
brother. The Episcopalian would most emphatically reject the one which the Lutheran would so
kindly give him. Thus each would feel about
the name chosen by his sectarian friend and
brother. Thank the Lord, none feels slandered or
abused when called a Christian or disciple of the
lowly Nazarene. Let us, then, accept the name
given to the bride by the Bridegroom himself,
and reject every other with disdain as the true
and loving bride of Christ, who is called the husband of the Church. Let us strive to call Bible
things by Bible names. The Church of God or
Church of Christ are Bible names.

When we can get rid of party names and party
creeds, the party spirit will soon die. There is
not one fact which God has given to be believed
as essential to salvation about which the religious
world has any controversy; not one command of
God given to be obeyed about which the religious
world is disagreed. The controversy is about
something else. Things believed or disbelieved,
which would neither shut a man out of heaven
nor let him in, are what (whether true or false, it
matters little) have been discussed until the spirituality of the church has well-nigh fled. That

faith in God and in Jesus Christ as his only begotten Son is needful to be believed none doubt for
a single moment. Whatever else may be required
by creeds, this truth alone has power to save the
soul. That the Spirit does convert by its facts,
control by its laws and comfort by its promises,
none will or can deny; that the Holy Spirit is
promised to every child of God as an indwelling
guest, a Comforter to abide with him forever, is
beyond dispute ; that every believing penitent or
regenerate person ought to be baptized has the
united testimony of all who acknowledge the di-
vinity of Christ and the inspiration of the Bible.
The dispute is whether the children of believing
parents shall be admitted to the divine ordinance.
No one denies that believing, penitent, baptized
persons have a perfect right to the Lord's house
and table. The question in dispute is whether
the unbaptized can claim the right. Every pro-
fessed child of God freely admits the privilege,
and it is the duty of every one to examine himself. It is only when one claims the right to
examine others that the spirit of controversy is
again aroused.

Once more, and I have done. The whole
religious world, in one grand army, lifts up
its voice with one accord, and says that the
believing, penitent, baptized person, who lives a
God-fearing, Christ-loving, alms-giving, devout
and prayerful life, will and must be saved. That
all such will be gathered with the blood-washed
throng at last in the peaceful and sinless city of
our God, where are palms of victory and crowns

of glory, fadeless and bright, even the Universalist himself does not dispute or doubt.   Thus we find the inspired Paul, in his letter to the church at Ephesus (chapter iv. 1–6), giving this pathetic and impressive exhortation : " That they walk worthy of their high and holy calling, in lowliness and meekness, with long-suffering, bearing with one another in love, endeavoring to keep the unity of the Spirit in the bond of peace."

" There is one body and one Spirit, one hope of your calling, one Lord, one faith, one baptism, one God and Father, who is over all, through all, and in all."   Here are the seven pillars planted by the Head of the Church, strong enough and broad enough for the Church of Christ to rest upon, and whilst the ages last " the gates of hades shall not prevail against it."   All who have the one faith, the one Lord, and have been baptized by the one baptism into the one body—Christ (Gal. iii. 27)—and, because in the one body (Gal. iv. 6), have received the one Spirit as a constant Comforter and an ever-abiding and indwelling guest, are the heirs of God and joint-heirs with Christ to an unfading and never-failing patrimony.

Do not, dear brother, barter such a claim for sectarian pottage, however palatable or delicious, but stand in the full liberty of the children of God and gospel of Christ, " contend earnestly for the faith once delivered to the saints," and when the Master comes you shall enter with him to the " marriage supper of the Lamb," to enjoy all God has promised to the faithful.

[Written at San Francisco, Cal.]

www.ingramcontent.com/pod-product-compliance
Lightning Source LLC
Chambersburg PA
CBHW021120020726
47500CB00003B/849